Praise for
JAMES PATTERSON

Praise for BECOMING MUHAMMAD ALI

"Cassius Clay's kinetic boyhood—depicted through prose, poetry, and illustration—is the prism through which this uplifting novel casts the myth of the legendary boxer."
—*New York Times*, **Best Children's Books of the Year**

"This utterly delightful story about Ali's childhood is a smash hit. Get this uplifting, informative book onto library shelves and into kids' hands."
—*School Library Journal*, **starred review**

"Patterson and Alexander, two heavyweights in the world of books, unite to tell the story of how Cassius Clay grew up to be Muhammad Ali, one of the greatest boxers of all time."
—*The Horn Book*, **starred review**

"The prose and poems reflect Clay's public bravado and private humbleness as well as his appreciation and respect for family and friends. A knockout!"
—*Booklist*, **starred review**

"Spare...witty...Cassius's narrative illustrates his charisma [and] drive...Powerful, accessible view of a fascinating figure."
—*Publishers Weekly*, **starred review**

"A stellar collaboration that introduces an important and intriguing individual to today's readers."
—*Kirkus Reviews*, **starred review**

"These lightning-bolt figures are poetry surrounded by prose...a kinetic, dazzling experience...Like the world many adolescents inhabit, the world that *Becoming Muhammad Ali* presents is complex...But most importantly, it's a reminder that once upon a time Cassius Clay, all poetry and italics, was a kid like the rest of us. It is my hope that Black children read this book, see themselves in young Clay, and know that they too are poetry made flesh."
—*New York Times Book Review*

Praise for the **MAXIMUM RIDE** Series

School's Out—Forever

"Readers are in for another exciting, wild ride."
—**Kirkus Reviews**

Praise for the **MIDDLE SCHOOL** Series

Middle School, The Worst Years of My Life

"A keen appreciation of kids' insecurities and an even more astute understanding of what might propel boy readers through a book...a perfectly pitched novel."

 —**Los Angeles Times**

"Cleverly delves into the events that make middle school so awkward: cranky bus drivers, tardy slips, bathroom passes, and lots of rules."
—**Associated Press**

Praise for the **JACKY HA-HA** Series

Jacky Ha-Ha

"A strong female protagonist, realistic characters, and a balanced approach to middle-school life make this book a winner."
—**Common Sense Media**

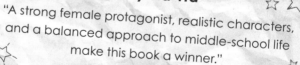

"James Patterson has figured out the formula for writing entertaining books for tween readers."
—**Parents' Choice**

Middle School

Middle School: The Worst Years of My Life
Middle School: Get Me Out of Here!
Middle School: Big Fat Liar
Middle School: How I Survived Bullies, Broccoli, and Snake Hill
Middle School: Ultimate Showdown
Middle School: Save Rafe!
Middle School: Just My Rotten Luck
Middle School: Dog's Best Friend
Middle School: Escape to Australia
Middle School: From Hero to Zero
Middle School: Born to Rock
Middle School: Master of Disaster
Middle School: Field Trip Fiasco
Middle School: It's a Zoo in Here!

Treasure Hunters

Treasure Hunters
Treasure Hunters: Danger Down the Nile
Treasure Hunters: Secret of the Forbidden City
Treasure Hunters: Peril at the Top of the World
Treasure Hunters: Quest for the City of Gold
Treasure Hunters: All-American Adventure
Treasure Hunters: The Plunder Down Under

Becoming Muhammad Ali (cowritten with Kwame Alexander)

Best Nerds Forever

Laugh Out Loud

Not So Normal Norbert

Pottymouth and Stoopid

Public School Superhero

Scaredy Cat

Unbelievably Boring Bart

Word of Mouse

For exclusives, trailers, and other information, visit jimmypatterson.org.

MIDDLE SCHOOL
IT'S A ZOO IN HERE!

JAMES PATTERSON

AND BRIAN SITTS
ILLUSTRATED BY JOMIKE TEJIDO

JIMMY Patterson Books
LITTLE, BROWN AND COMPANY
NEW YORK • BOSTON

Copyright © 2022 by James Patterson
Illustrations by Jomike Tejido

Cover art by Jomike Tejido. Cover image of bars © CG_dmitriy/Shutterstock.com.
Cover design by Liam Donnelly. Cover copyright © 2022 by Hachette Book Group, Inc.

JIMMY Patterson Books / Little, Brown and Company
Hachette Book Group
1290 Avenue of the Americas, New York, NY 10104
JamesPatterson.com

First Edition: January 2022

JIMMY Patterson Books is an imprint of Little, Brown and Company, a division of Hachette Book Group, Inc. The Little, Brown name and logo are trademarks of Hachette Book Group, Inc.
The JIMMY Patterson Books® name and logo are trademarks of JBP Business, LLC.

The publisher is not responsible for websites (or their content) that are not owned by the publisher.

Library of Congress Cataloging-in-Publication Data
Names: Patterson, James, 1947– author. | Sitts, Brian, author. | Tejido, Jomike, illustrator.
Title: It's a zoo in here! / James Patterson and Brian Sitts; illustrated by Jomike Tejido.
Other titles: It is a zoo in here
Description: First edition. | New York : Jimmy Patterson Books/Little, Brown and Company, 2022. | Series: Middle school ; 14 | Audience: Ages 8–12. | Summary: Rafe Khatchadorian is horrified that because of a missed science assignment he has to go to summer school; but instead of three weeks in a school room, he finds himself as a volunteer at BushyTail animal refuge, which is really hard, smelly work—and somehow he needs to use the experience (and the help of a girl he meets there) to produce a first-class science report.
Identifiers: LCCN 2021040288 | ISBN 9780316430081 (hardcover) | ISBN 9780316430319 (ebook)
Subjects: LCSH: Zoos—Juvenile fiction. | Zoo animals—Juvenile fiction. | Animal welfare—Juvenile fiction. | Middle schools—Juvenile fiction. | Friendship—Juvenile fiction. | Humorous stories. | CYAC: Zoos—Fiction. | Zoo animals—Fiction. | Animal welfare—Fiction. | Middle schools—Fiction. | Schools—Fiction. | Friendship—Fiction. | Humorous stories. | LCGFT: Humorous fiction.
Classification: LCC PZ7.P27653 It 2022 | DDC 813.54 [Fic]—dc23
LC record available at https://lccn.loc.gov/2021040288

ISBNs: 978-0-316-43008-1 (hardcover), 978-0-316-43031-9 (ebook)

Printed in the United States of America

LSC-H

Printing 1, 2021

MIDDLE SCHOOL

SCHOOL

IT'S A ZOO IN HERE!

CHAPTER 1

NO MORE TEACHER'S DIRTY LOOKS!

Wahoo!"

It was the last minute of the last day of school before summer vacation. Could anything be sweeter? Not for yours truly! Because I'm Rafe Khatchadorian. And if you've heard (or read) anything about me, you already know that Hills Village Middle School is probably my least-favorite place in the whole universe. There are a lot of reasons for that, most of which are *not* my fault. Really. Ask my friends.

Okay, *friend*. I'm working on bumping that up to plural.

Sometimes I just get frustrated by stupid rules, like "No parkour in class." And sometimes I get carried away by my own crazy ideas, like painting a mural of the Story of Man on the ceiling of the boys' bathroom. I heard there was a wanted poster with my face on it in the faculty lounge. Probably just a rumor.

On the last day of the semester, it was good-bye to all that! I couldn't wait to escape! And I really, truly thought I was home free.

But as usual, I counted my chickens too soon. If you spend a little time with me, you'll see that my very best days have a way of turning into, well... something else!

My last big task for the year was cleaning out my hall locker. And I'll be honest, it got ugly in there! Way in the back, on the top shelf, I found a plastic bag of hard-boiled eggs from last September. At least I *think* they were eggs. Hard to tell with all the green, furry stuff. Then I pulled out a wadded-up gym shirt that hadn't seen the inside of a washer since January. The stench pretty much cleared the corridor.

I also dug out a few long-lost library books (two dollars in fines), a petrified Glorp bar, an old Voldemort Halloween mask, a flyer from our class production of *Les Miz* (spoiler: it was pretty miserable), and some Machismo body spray. Probably seemed like a smart purchase at the time.

But now all that was behind me! All my earthly possessions were stuffed into my backpack and I was dreaming about the three worry-free months ahead of me…

"Ready, Rafe-ster?" It was my friend Flip Savage, one of the funniest kids on the planet.

"I've never been readier."

Me and Flip always walk out together on the last day of school. It's a tradition. Our other tradition: taking a few happy moments to vote on which teacher we're going to miss the *least*! This year, there were some really solid contenders. For starters, our first-period language arts teacher, Ms. Loring.

"*Loring*. Rhymes with *boring*!" said Flip. Couldn't have said it better myself.

We also discussed Mr. Filbert, from third-period social studies. His George Washington impression really got on our nerves. Especially the part when he tried to eat a peach with his wooden teeth. And obviously we had to consider Mrs. Frecht, the Spanish teacher with the German accent. *Nein comprendo.*

But in the end, it was no contest. The winner by a mile was Mr. Manta, our fifth-period science teacher—aka the A-less Wonder. The last time anybody got higher than a B+ in his class was... *never*! Not that science is my strong suit anyway.

You've probably picked up on the fact that I'm more of an artist at heart. I passed Mr. Manta's final by the skin of my teeth.

"Farewell, heredity charts!" I yelled down the hall.

"So long, ecological cycles!" yelled Flip, even louder.

We picked up the pace, passing the gym, the scene of so many painful moments, and then the cafeteria, the site of this year's infamous Meatloaf Rebellion. We turned one more corner and then we saw it—the light at the end of the tunnel!

Actually, just the door at the end of the hallway. But it meant the same thing. I was finally done! Sprung! *Summer, here I come!*

But suddenly, a shadow loomed over us, blocking our way. Blocking the hall.

Blocking the door. Blocking the sun.

"Mr. Khatchadorian? A moment, please."

CHAPTER 2

NOT SO FAST!

It was Mr. Manta in the flesh—and that's a lot of flesh. Mr. Manta is a big guy, with a huge head and hands the size of hams. In one of those hammy hands, he was dangling a document with a Hills Village logo at the top. Very official-looking.

"Mr. Khatchadorian," said Mr. Manta, "are you aware that a report on amphibian development was due in April?"

My head was spinning. "Amphibian development?" Sounded vaguely familiar.

"You mean polliwogs?" asked Flip.

"Tadpoles," said Mr. Manta, leaning over me. "You seem to be missing your tadpole report. And without it, your transcript is incomplete." The way he said "incomplete" was like a dagger to my happiness.

At this point, Flip gave me a sad little wave and backed off down the hall. There went my wingman. Now it was just Me vs. Manta. I didn't like those odds.

I wracked my brain. *Think, Rafe, think!* I clearly remembered the tadpoles wiggling around in their little glass petri dishes, going nowhere fast. Flip and I even gave them names. Captain Marvel. Thor. Black Widow. But a *report*? I had to admit, I had zero memory of handing one in.

"Maybe it was the week I was home with head lice," I said. I thought head lice were way more interesting than tadpoles. But I didn't say so.

"No matter the reason," said Mr. Manta, "you're short two credits in science. And I think you know what that means."

Unfortunately, I *did* know what it meant. The Hammer of Doom. The Unthinkable. The Worst of the Worst. But until Mr. Manta actually said the words, I couldn't believe it.

"Mr. Khatchadorian—I'll see you in summer school."

My vacation was over before it even started. Again.

The Summer Slayer

CHAPTER 3

THE WALK OF SHAME

You know those movie scenes where everything gets foggy around the edges and the music gets really weird—like some guy banging on piano strings with a mallet? That's what it was like on my walk home. At least that's how it sounded in my head.

This couldn't be happening again—could it? Whatever déjà vu is, I was feeling it. Because when it comes to summer school, this wasn't my first rodeo.

Awhile back, Mom sent me to a summer school/ summer camp called Camp Wannamorra. It was a mix of actual schoolwork and "summer activities." Mom promised it was going to be fun. And you know what, it kinda *was*. (It even turned into a bestselling book!)

You'll love this story—
after you're done with
the one you're reading!

But this...was not that.

Summer school for science meant being stuck with Mr. Manta in a dull classroom with no air conditioning, staring at tadpoles through a magnifying glass, recording their growth patterns on graph paper, and then entering those measurements into a computer program called FrogStat. In other words: the exact *opposite* of fun.

It was humiliating. I was feeling about two feet tall—which is about a foot shorter than I usually feel. By the time I got home, I was slumped over so far my chin practically scraped the sidewalk. My dog, Junior, ran out to get his usual belly-rub greeting, but I could only manage a pat on his furry head. I didn't want to see anybody. I didn't want to talk to anybody. I especially didn't want to...

"SURPRISE!!!"

CHAPTER 4

PARTY ON!

Leave it to my mom to put together a last-minute end-of-school family celebration. Normally, I would *love* that. But under the circumstances, I just wanted to crawl under a rock.

I guess I got home a little early, because the preparations were still underway. Grandma Dotty was setting out red paper plates and white plastic forks while my super-annoying kid sister, Georgia, pointed out the environmental risks.

"You know plastic is destroying the oceans, right, Grandma?" Georgia has a way of letting the air out of any balloon.

"It's just one little party, dear," said Dotty. "But if you prefer, I'll eat with my hands."

"Hey, Rafe! Happy summer! Another big year behind you!" said Mom as she came out of the kitchen with a white cardboard box that could only mean one thing: a free pie from her job at Swifty's Diner. In case you haven't heard, Swifty's pies are world-class.

"It's your favorite," Mom said. And when she opened the lid, I could see that she was right. Chocolate Cream with Cookie Crumbles. This pie belonged in the National Pie Hall of Fame—and I would be honored to make the induction speech. But not today.

As soon as she noticed my slump, Mom knew something was wrong. She has a patented, fail-proof, built-in Rafe Depression Detector (RDD), and I was setting it off big-time.

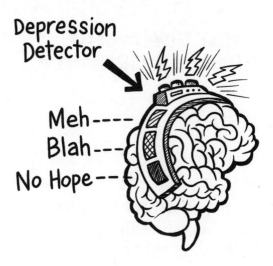

Depression Detector

Meh----

Blah---

No Hope--

I couldn't even look at her. I just handed her the slip I got from Mr. Manta.

"Summer school?" she said. "Rafe, you've got to be *kidding*!"

But then I heard something *truly* shocking, especially since it was coming from my brainiac kid sister:

"That makes *two* of us!"

CHAPTER 5

THAT'S HOW THE CRUMBLES CRUMBLE

Summer school for Georgia? That was impossible—unless she flushed one of Principal Stricker's pet hermit crabs down the toilet. If you know anything about Georgia (and nobody knows her like I do), you know she has never missed a school assignment in her annoyingly high-achieving life!

"Summer school? *You?*" I asked.

"Not as a *student*, dummy," she said. "As a *tutor*! They asked me to be a Math Mentor for sixth graders, and they're paying me five dollars an hour!"

Great. Just great. I didn't think there could be

anything worse than summer school. But it turned
out there was: having my kid sister rub my nose in
it every single day—while she got filthy, stinking
rich.

"Who wants pie?"

Grandma was trying to lighten the mood with sweets, but it was no use. For me, even the cookie crumbles had lost their crunch. I excused myself and headed for the Fortress of Solitude—aka my bedroom. Junior followed me, leaving behind a party-size bowl of Canine Crispy Crackers.

"Sleep well, loser," said Georgia.

I closed the door and flopped facedown on my pillow. Let the tadpole nightmares begin.

CHAPTER 6

A MAN AND A PLAN

Two minutes later…

Knock, knock.

Clearly, my DO NOT DISTURB UNDER PENALTY OF DEATH sign wasn't working.

Junior was curled up with me on the bed—even though he knows he's supposed to be sleeping in his doggy bed on the floor. But I guess he understood that I needed a little extra comfort. He even reached up with his paws to give *me* a belly rub.

Sometimes I get the feeling that I'm *his* pet instead of the other way around.

Knock, knock!

"Go away!" I yelled with my face buried in the pillow. But my words fell on deaf ears. I heard

the door creak open and I could tell right away
that it was Mom. She still wore her rubber-soled
shoes from work, and they always squeak in a
certain way. Usually I love that sound. But now I
just wanted to be alone with my dark, amphibious
thoughts.

I felt my mattress sink a few inches as Mom
sat down on the edge of my bed. Now, you need
to know that I really, truly love my mother. She
might be my favorite person in the whole world.
And she can usually make me feel better about
almost anything. But this was no ordinary thing.

This was summer school. It meant going back to the place I hate most—the scene of my biggest embarrassments.

And this was just one more. Add it to the list of Rafe's Biggest Mess-Ups. (It's a pretty long list.) This situation was beyond even Mom's healing powers.

But Julia Khatchadorian isn't the type to give up without a fight.

"Rafe, I know you're frustrated. And I understand. I wish this hadn't happened. But in the scheme of life, this is a speed bump, not a disaster."

"Easy for you to say," I wanted to say. It sure felt like a disaster to me.

I heard the sound of a plastic plate sliding onto my night table.

"I brought you a slice of chocolate pie."

"Thanks, Mom," I said. "But I'm really not hungry."

"Okay then," she said. "You get some rest." I felt her lift off my mattress. "We've got a big appointment tomorrow."

Appointment? I wondered what she had in

store for me. Some quality time with Dr. Payne, my molar-mauling dentist? Or a date with my barber, Eduardo, who thinks bowl cuts are still in style? As it turned out, none of the above.

It was even worse.

As Mom closed the door, she said, "We have a meeting...with Mr. Manta."

The last person on earth I wanted to see.

CHAPTER 7

IN THE BELLY OF THE BEAST

I'd never been inside Mr. Manta's office before. Most of my spare time was spent in Principal Stricker's office (on an involuntary basis). This room was really tiny. The desk looked like doll furniture with Mr. Manta crammed behind it. There were books on animal biology all over the place and a few old *National Geographic* nature posters on the walls. One camel. One grizzly bear. And a flock of seagulls. On the shelf behind Mr. Manta's desk, there was some kind of preserved furry critter, frozen in place with its mouth wide open and its little paws raised.

Ferret? Gerbil? Meerkat?

Snack? No, thanks— I'm stuffed!

"My goodness! Is that a *mongoose*?" Mom asked with amazement. She never ceases to amaze me. I could tell Mr. Manta was impressed.

"Well done, Mrs. Khatchadorian," said Mr. Manta. "Very few people know that."

"Please, call me Jules."

And then it was down to business. According to Mr. Manta, the missing tadpole report was serious stuff. He started babbling about state mandates, assessment rubrics, blah blah blah. First my eyes glazed over, then my ears. But Mom looked really interested. She leaned in and nodded her head at everything Mr. Manta was saying. She totally agreed with him about how important animal studies were to a rigorous middle school curriculum. Before I knew it, they were talking about the wildlife drawings Mom did as an art student.

What's going on here? My own mother was bonding with the enemy! *What's her game?*

Wait.

Did I actually see Mr. Manta crack a little smile? That was a first.

"So, Rafe—do you like animals too?" asked

Mr. Manta. Was that a trick question? What self-respecting kid doesn't like animals? I even ran my own dog-walking service. But that's another story. In fact, it's another whole book!

Read how Rafe
really stepped in it!

"Sure I do," I said. "But tadpoles aren't really animals, are they?" I felt Mom give me a little kick under the chair.

"Rafe," said Mr. Manta, "I can tell that your mother really cares about your studies. And I know that spending your summer in a hot classroom is not a very pleasant prospect."

That was the understatement of the century.

But I still had no idea where this was going. Mr. Manta leaned forward and folded his ham-hands on the desk.

"I have a proposal for you," he said.

"Okay," I said. My eyes and ears were now fully open.

"What if, instead of your spending three weeks here in school doing a tadpole lab, I were to let you do an independent study project, like your mother suggested?"

"Like what?" I asked. Was this some kind of trick?

"It would be outdoors. With real animals."

Now I perked up. I saw a sliver of daylight. I sat up really straight.

"No summer school?" I glanced over at Mom. She looked totally serious, but she had a little twinkle in her eye.

"Think of it as summer *work*," said Mr. Manta. "I still want a report. But it can be on any animal you choose."

"But where?" I asked. My mind was spinning. The zoo? The dog park? Our backyard?

"Actually," said Mr. Manta, "I have a very special place in mind." He reached into his top desk drawer and pulled out a business card. He slid it across the desk toward me. I picked it up.

The card said BUSHYTAIL ANIMAL REFUGE. There was a drawing of a paw print behind the name, and below it was a slogan: WHERE ANIMALS GET BACK ON THEIR FEET.

"I promise you, Rafe," said Mr. Manta, "these are animals you will never forget!"

CHAPTER 8

MENAGERIE OF MISFITS

Almost there, Rafe!"

Just two days later, Mom drove me to work on my first day as an official BushyTail volunteer. Emphasis on *volunteer*. Unlike Georgia, I wasn't earning a penny for my summer efforts. But I still owed Mom a huge debt. I have no idea how she swayed Mr. Manta, but she sure knew how to speak his language. And at least I was out in the fresh air instead of being cooped up in a classroom. If you ask me, my mom should be Mother of the Year, every year—just for helping me out of tough spots. I know I don't thank her enough, but I'm not too good with mushy stuff.

"Hey, Mom…" I said as we turned onto a dirt road.

"You're welcome," she said.

That's another thing I love about Mom. She knows what I want to say before I even say it.

We drove through an entrance with a big sign that said BUSHYTAIL ANIMAL REFUGE—ANIMALS WELCOME ANYTIME. HUMANS, CALL AHEAD. My new boss was waiting inside, wearing orange bib overalls, a straw hat, and rubber boots. As soon as Mom pulled the car to a stop, he walked over to the passenger-side window and grunted.

"Morning. Name's Penrod Pincus."

As usual, Mom piped right up.

"I'm Jules Khatchadorian, Mr. Pincus—and this is my son, Rafe." Awkward pause. Then I felt Mom poke me in the ribs.

"Hello, Mr. Pincus," I said. "Nice to meet you." I held my hand out for a shake, but Mr. Pincus was already walking off.

"Let's go. Work to do," he grunted.

I hopped out of the car. Mom blew me a little good-luck kiss.

"Be good, Rafe!" she said. "I'll pick you up after work!" She turned the Khatchadorianmobile around and headed off to her morning shift at Swifty's.

Mr. Pincus had already unlatched a huge metal gate that led to the inner part of the compound. Now he was holding it open. I double-timed it to catch up.

I observed a couple of things about my new boss right away. First, he grunted.

For sure, there were some words mixed in. But grunting was his main thing. Short grunts. Long grunts. High grunts. Low grunts. A whole glossary of grunts. Second, he didn't like to wait around. Always on the move.

Once we passed through the main gate, I started hearing and seeing and smelling things that had my senses doing cartwheels. This was not your everyday petting zoo. There were no cute pens with lambs and baby rabbits. The website said BushyTail was "a fully licensed open-air animal rehabilitation refuge." In other words, it was the last stop for animals nobody else wanted or knew what to do with. They came from circuses, state parks, puppy mills, aquariums—from all over. Sometimes the animals just got dropped off at the gate with a note, like a fruit basket.

I followed (more like ran after) Mr. Pincus as
he led the way around the compound, which was
huge—about the size of three soccer fields! I could
hardly see the end of it. There was a tall wire fence
that ran around the whole thing. I wondered if it was
electrified. (Note to self: Don't touch it to find out.)

Mr. Pincus had a special grunt for each animal
and a little story about how it got there. Our first
stop was a medium-size pool filled with salt water.
Inside was a sea turtle named Eight Ball. Strange
name, right? Here's the story:

Somehow the little guy got a plastic six-pack
ring wrapped around his shell when he was a
hatchling. As he grew, the ring squeezed his shell
into a figure eight.

On top of that, a barracuda nipped off one of his

flippers, so he could only swim in circles. All things considered, he looked pretty happy. The BushyTail pool was a lot smaller than the Pacific Ocean, but it was a lot safer too. With free turtle food thrown in!

Next door, in a fenced-in area, was Gilbert the goat. He was doing time for eating the Baby Jesus from the Hills Village Nativity display. I guess the security-cam footage made it an open-and-shut case. Mr. Pincus says goats will eat pretty much anything. He warned me not to drop my cell phone.

"Arf!"

Out of nowhere, a big yellow Lab ran up and started sniffing all around Mr. Pincus's overalls. Turns out, this dog had a pretty interesting resume. His name was Sulfur. He used to be in training to be a drug-sniffing canine, but he washed out because he only barked at the smell of farts. Very particular nose. He had a special attraction to Mr. Pincus, for reasons I would soon understand.

"Arf!"

Let me pause right here. I think I'm a pretty good describer, but words alone can't do justice to BushyTail. Here's a drone's-eye view of the whole complex, just the way I remember it.

snacks

BUSHYTAIL
Animal compound

Entry Tickets Exit

MAIN
ENTRANCE

Now that you've got the picture, you can see why the whole tour took almost an hour. But Mr. Pincus never stopped to rest. Not once! As for me, my legs were out of shape from sitting behind a desk for the past nine months, so I was definitely feeling some aches and pains toward the end. But I sucked it up. I wasn't going to let an old guy in overalls outrun me.

I was kind of wondering when Mr. Pincus was going to ask about what brought me here. Or explain how he knew Mr. Manta. Or inquire about my interests and hobbies. But nope. None of that. Mr. Pincus had a one-track mind. I got the feeling that he was a lot more interested in animals than people.

Of course, since it was my first day, I figured he was probably going to take it easy on me after the tour—maybe treat me to a nice lunch, or even let me off early.

But I figured wrong.

CHAPTER 9

TOO MUCH MONKEY BUSINESS

When we came to a little metal shed, Mr. Pincus reached in and handed me a pair of rubber boots and a hard hat. Kinda cool. Then he handed me a big bucket and a shovel. Not so cool. Then he pointed the way to my first assignment: cleaning out the chimp enclosure. Not cool at all!

On TV and in the movies, chimps look friendly and fun, right? But trust me, you never really know an animal until you have to clean up after it.

The chimp compound was a big rectangle with a low wooden hut and a few dead trees propped up for climbing. There were eight or nine chimps sitting around and hanging from the branches. The grown-up chimps puffed their chests and scratched their butts. A few really cute baby chimps rode

on their mothers' backs. When I walked in, the
grown-ups made screeching sounds and rocked
back and forth. It sounded like a real-life nature
documentary, but I couldn't shake the feeling that
they were all laughing at me. The sound was pretty
loud. But the *smell* was something else.

Imagine taking a deep whiff from a bottle of
ammonia. (Don't do it. Just imagine it!) Now add
an overtone of musk, rotten fruit, and wet fur.
That will get you close to what I was up against.
I wondered why Mr. Pincus didn't give me nose
plugs. Phew! Ugh! The faster I got *this* job done,
the better.

I put the shovel blade down and started to
scrape, scoop, and dump. Scrape, scoop, dump.
Scrape, scoop, dump. Pretty soon, the bucket was
filling up. And so were my nostrils.

All of a sudden…ZING! Something whizzed past my ear! ZING! PING!

Now it was raining little pellets all around. At first I thought the chimps were throwing pebbles at me. Rude.

Then I realized they weren't pebbles. It was poop!

Duck, Rafe, duck! Maybe this was a traditional form of chimp greeting. I wondered if I should throw something back. Anyway, it's a good thing I was wearing a hard hat!

I finished scooping while the air assault continued. The bucket was almost overflowing now. Pretty gross. Out of the corner of my eye, I saw Mr. Pincus walking along the path outside the enclosure. He was leading a group of little kids on a tour, grunting all the way. The kids all wore bright-yellow T-shirts saying HAPPY HILLS DAY CAMP. The kids stopped and started pointing at me. They were laughing hysterically. I guess poop-pelting is pretty funny when you're not the one being pelted.

As the kids walked away down the path, one chubby camper hung behind to finish off his Jumbo Scooter Bar. There was a big trash container about three feet away clearly marked DO NOT LITTER! Plain as day. But the kid took his last bite, licked his fat little fingers, and dropped the wrapper right on the ground! Unbelievable. What's up with kids these days? Good thing Georgia wasn't around. She would have made a citizen's arrest.

Mr. Pincus caught my eye, then pointed at the wrapper. I nodded. Got it. As if the chimps weren't bad enough, it looked like I had to clean up after humans too.

CHAPTER 10

THE LAY OF THE LAND

That first day was kind of a trial by fire.
Actually, more like a trial by poop. I think
maybe Mr. Pincus gave me the stinkiest job to start
with just so he could see what I was made of, and
I guess he saw some kind of promise. Till then,
my animal experience was pretty much limited to
dogs, cats, and tadpoles. But there was something
about working with the wild animals at BushyTail
that I really liked. It was exciting and confusing at
the same time, if that makes any sense.

It took me a few days to get oriented to the
whole layout, which was kind of like a maze. I don't
think there was any real plan to the way it was
set up. It seemed like the place just started small
and kept on growing, like a weed. And the more

animals Mr. Pincus took in—which happened all the time—the more confusing things got. There were fences and bushes and hedgerows and twisty trails everywhere.

As soon as I thought I knew where I was going, another path popped up to confuse me. Mr. Pincus wasn't big on signs. So I learned to navigate by sounds and smells. Turn right at the howl. Go left at the stench.

This was all pretty new to me. To tell you the truth, I've never been what you'd call outdoorsy. Like I said before, I'm more the artistic type. Picture a kid drawing robot invaders with a flashlight under the covers after bedtime. That's me. But at BushyTail, I started to feel my primal instincts coming to life. My senses were on high alert. I was totally aware of my surroundings every second. I got so in tune with nature I thought about changing my name to Tarzan Khatchadorian. But that would mean getting new labels in all my underwear. Never mind.

Even when I got most of the place mapped out in my head, there were still some mystery areas at the far end of the compound I hadn't explored. Was

I curious? You bet. But no time to worry about that now—I had plenty to keep me busy. And each day, there were surprises around every corner, such as:

A parrot who watched too many soap operas.

A boa constrictor with two heads.

A pair of boxing kangaroos.

Some animals were so strange I never even knew they existed. Ever heard of a capybara? Me neither—until I got here. Imagine your favorite pet guinea pig, then supersize it until it's about ten times bigger.

Mr. Pincus says capybaras are the largest rodents in the world, and I guess he should know. He rescued a whole family of them from a guy in Miami who was about to turn them into fur coats.

Capybaras eat grass and sometimes their own poop, which is basically like eating the same grass twice. Pretty efficient when you think about it.

"To each his own," Mr. Pincus says. I try not to judge.

Pretty soon, I learned which animals were friendly and which ones were afraid of people, which ones liked to nuzzle, and which ones got nippy. Mr. Pincus said a lot of the rescue animals had been treated badly in their previous lives— so I couldn't blame them for being afraid of humans. I learned to tell the early birds from the late sleepers. (We in the animal business call them nocturnals.) I learned how to spot lizards when they were camouflaged in leaves. Even the chameleon couldn't fool me.

By the end of my first week, I could hear the difference between a toucan and a macaw. I learned to never walk up to Stripes the zebra from the rear, to avoid getting kicked. I knew how to hold an apple in my hand to feed Molly the mule— palm flat, fingers straight—to avoid losing a finger. All valuable life lessons that I would never have gotten from sitting in summer school. But there was something else too. I was starting to feel like the animals kind of depended on me. And that was a pretty great feeling.

CHAPTER 11

WHERE RAFE GETS GOOSED!

Honk! Honk!"

"Ouch!"

Once again, I was daydreaming and walked too close to the goose pond. I should have learned my lesson by now. This was a real danger zone! Every single time I got near it, Mother Goose ran out and tried to peck a hole in the seat of my pants. I learned that geese are very territorial. And those big webbed feet can move a lot faster than you think!

Every morning when I got to the BushyTail office, Mr. Pincus was already there sipping his coffee and chomping on a huge breakfast bean burrito. And when I say huge, I mean the size of a rolled-up towel. The burrito came back to haunt everybody later in the day—but Sulfur the fart-sniffing dog always gave us fair warning.

Sometimes Mr. Pincus said, "Mornin'," which I assume was short for "Good morning, Rafe! So nice to see you! I hope you had a restful night!" But mostly, he just grunted and pointed to a whiteboard with a list of my tasks for the day.

- Wash donkeys.
- Collect ants for anteater.
- Pick up ostrich feathers.
- Give beavers more logs.
- Groom hedgehog. (Wear gloves!)
(Watch out for missing tarantula. Answers to "Terry.")

I soon figured out that a big part of a BushyTail volunteer's job was lugging food. Pails of grain. Bales of hay. Buckets of slugs. And I discovered one of the basic laws of the animal kingdom: once you bring an animal something to eat, you've got a friend for life. It was the same for every species— from aardvarks to zebus. Pretty soon, I had them all eating out of the palm of my hand!

But there was one job so amazingly cool, I can't *believe* I got to do it. And that I messed it up so, so badly.

CHAPTER 12

LeMUR LOVe!

My favorite day yet—by *far*—was the first day I got to feed the lemurs! Mr. Pincus led the way to the lemur enclosure, handed me a pail, and grunted. Then he fastened the gate behind me and walked off down the path. By now, I guess he kind of trusted me. Believe me, that's going to cause huge problems later in this story, but I don't want to get ahead of myself. For the moment, I was in heaven.

Are you a movie fan? I am. Especially the *Madagascar* movies. I've seen them all about ten times. Of all the characters, the lemurs are my favorites. And this was like meeting the cast! Turns out, they're even cuter in person. Real-life lemurs have big brown eyes, soft gray fur, and thick black tails with white stripes (or maybe it's the other way around).

I stood near the entrance for a minute and then kind of tiptoed in, so I wouldn't scare them away. Lemurs can be a little skittish at first.

The whole place was filled with craggy rocks and logs. There were thick ropes strung from one side to the other, and a bunch of thick metal bars overhead. These guys had their own deluxe jungle gym! I was kind of jealous. This setup was *way* cooler than my school's lame play equipment, which looked like it'd been designed by drunken pirates.

The lemurs got pretty excited when they saw me coming, jumping from rock to rock and balancing on the ropes and bars like furry acrobats. I had a feeling I was about to become their favorite homo sapiens because I was bringing them their favorite lunch in the world—crunchy, delicious dead crickets. Yum!

I sat down on a rock and put the pail of crickets in my lap. As soon as the lemurs realized that I was a food source and not an alpha predator, they started hopping in my direction. They were sniffing the air and bobbing their heads and twitching their tails. "Adorbs!" as Georgia would say.

I put a dead cricket in my palm and one of the lemurs grabbed it with his paws, which look a lot like tiny hands—only hairier. That broke the ice. Pretty soon, I was practically *covered* in lemurs. They were hanging on my shoulders and climbing onto my head. But mostly they crawled into my lap to grab cricket after cricket. A little lightbulb went on in my head. Maybe I'd do my animal report on *lemurs*!

"Whoa! Slow down, guys!" I said.

The lemurs were plowing through crickets like popcorn at the multiplex. I was starting to wish I'd brought more, but Mr. Pincus was all about portion control. I guess a lean lemur is a healthy lemur.

Two baby lemurs pushed each other out of the way trying to get to my pail. That's when I heard it—the telltale sound of the BushyTail golf cart. It was kind of a low hum, with a sad little whine when it went uphill. Mr. Pincus sat behind the wheel, bouncing toward me. He drove so crazy I thought he might pop a wheelie—or flip over into the frog lagoon. Either one would have been pretty funny.

Instead, he pulled up to the front of the lemur enclosure and started waving his arms and grunting.

By now, I was actually starting to be able to interpret his noises. This one meant "Drop everything and come quick!"

I dropped the crickets.

CHAPTER 13

BiG PiNK

I hopped into the driver's seat next to Mr. Pincus and reached for the seat belt. Except there wasn't one. So I held on to the steering wheel for dear life. By now, it was about ten in the morning and the daily Pincus burrito was already working its magic. Good thing the golf cart was open-air. Sulfur would have been barking his head off.

On foot, going from the lemur lounge to the main gate took about five minutes. In the golf cart, we got there in about thirty seconds. Good thing there were no Hills Village cops around. We would've gotten a speeding ticket for sure.

When we pulled up to the front gate, I looked

around to see what all the fuss was about. Everything looked normal to me, except I could see that somebody had left a lawn ornament lying near the entrance. It was one of those big pink flamingos—the kind people stick in their yards next to a family of garden gnomes.

"Hey, Mr. Pincus," I said, walking over to it, "that'll look great in front of the office!"

I felt Mr. Pincus grab me by my BushyTail shirt collar and hold me back. Right about then, I noticed that the lawn ornament was twitching. It was alive!

"Never touch an injured bird," said Mr. Pincus. "They go right for the eyes!"

Holy smokes! I could have been blinded in one peck. Maybe two. But now what?

Before I had time to come up with a flamingo rescue plan, I heard the roar of an engine—a real one this time, not a golf cart. I saw a bright green Jeep zooming from the main road toward the BushyTail entrance. It sped through the main gate. Then it screeched to a stop and kicked up a bunch of dust. Pretty dramatic. I'd never seen this Jeep before. It wasn't the health inspector, or the zebra wrangler, or the farmer who collected our extra manure.

Mr. Pincus waved at the driver. "The vet's here!" he said.

The Jeep door popped open and a very tall woman stepped out. She wore a safari shirt with the sleeves rolled up, and her muscles bulged underneath. She had squinty lines in the corners of her eyes. Her hair was in a bun on top of her head, with a little stick holding it in place. The sign on the door of the Jeep said DARIA DEERWIN, DVM.

Dr. Deerwin didn't waste any time. She didn't even bother to say hi to Mr. Pincus. As soon as she spotted the flamingo, she walked toward it. Slowwwwly.

"Shhh, baby! It's okay..." For such a strong-looking woman, she had a really soft, soothing voice. At least when she talked to flamingos. The bird started flapping its wings and poking its beak in her direction. Dr. Deerwin stopped and held still. She turned her head back toward us.

"You!" she said. She meant me. "There's a small

blanket in the backseat of the Jeep. Bring it here!" This voice was not soothing at all. It was totally take-charge.

I walked toward the Jeep, trying not to make any sudden movements. I didn't want anybody's eyeballs getting pecked out on my account. Once I got to the Jeep, I reached for the back door and pulled the handle. When the door swung open, I jumped back! Two eyes were staring back at me from the other side! There was a voice attached.

"Y-Y-You g-g-get the blanket. I'll g-g-grab the g-g-goggles!"

It was a girl. Snapshot impression: about my age. Hair in short braids. Round face. Tiny stud in her right nostril. That was about all I could see before she closed the door on her side and disappeared. I grabbed the blanket that was lying on the backseat. The girl moved around the front of the Jeep. She wore a khaki shirt and matching shorts, like a uniform. With the goggles, she looked like a hybrid of an action figure and a science nerd.

The girl tossed the second pair of goggles to Dr. Deerwin. She caught them without even looking! Dr. Deerwin put the goggles on, then held her arm out toward me, wiggling her fingers. She wanted the blanket. I handed it to her.

The girl moved up slowly until she was right next to Dr. Deerwin. Then they moved together—on tiptoe—toward the flamingo. Goggle Girl's head only came up to Dr. Deerwin's belt. Dr. Deerwin held the blanket stretched out in front of her. The flamingo was flailing around and kicking with one leg, spinning itself in circles in the dirt. I could tell it really wanted to fly away, but that wasn't going to happen.

When Dr. Deerwin got about three feet away from the flamingo, she threw the blanket forward with a little flicking motion, kind of like tossing a Frisbee. Bingo! Right on target. The blanket landed on top of the bird's head and covered up half its body.

The second the blanket landed, the girl pounced!
She skidded hard on her bare knees right next to
the flamingo. After she wrapped the blanket softly
around its head, she put her arms underneath and
lifted it like a baby. Then she pulled it close to her
chest and whispered. I couldn't hear what she was
saying, but it must have worked because the big
pink bird calmed right down.

Mr. Pincus was grunting the whole time. As
for me—ever see a cartoon where a guy has his
mouth hanging open because he can't believe what
he's seeing? That's pretty much how I must have
looked.

100 percent accurate
representation

Goggle Girl handed the flamingo to Dr.
Deerwin, very gently. They were a pretty amazing
team. I had no idea what was going to happen
next, but I was hooked for sure. This was better
than reality TV. This was *reality*!

Mr. Pincus led the way to a small building
next to the main office. I'd only seen it from the
outside. It was white brick with small windows.
Dr. Deerwin followed right behind. I could see one
of the flamingo's legs dangling from under the
blanket. It looked like a pinkish-whitish stick, and
it was bent at a weird angle in the middle.

"You c-c-coming?"

Goggle Girl was talking to me. I think my
mouth was still hanging open. But somehow I
managed to say, "Yes. Coming!"

I had to jog a few steps to catch up to her.
She moved fast.

"I'm Rafe," I said.

"I'm P-P-Penelope. Nice to m-m-meet you."

I had about a hundred questions I wanted to ask Penelope, starting with where she learned how to capture flamingos. But, as you might have heard, talking to girls has never been my strong suit. I even get nervous around girls I know in school—and they're mostly normal. I had never, *ever* met a girl like Penelope.

For some reason, I felt like I was turning as pink as a flamingo. And my heart was beating like crazy. I remember thinking it must be all the excitement. What else could it be?

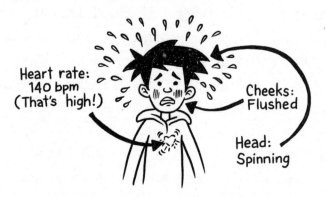

Heart rate: 140 bpm (That's high!)

Cheeks: Flushed

Head: Spinning

"Is Dr. Deerwin your boss?" I asked.

"Yep," she said. "Also my m-m-mom."

CHAPTER 14

A LEG TO STAND ON

Inside the clinic, the flamingo was lying on a soft blanket on top of a steel table—the kind they have in hospitals. And that's pretty much what this was. A hospital for animals. Penelope held the blanket gently over the flamingo's head while Dr. Deerwin examined its skinny leg.

"Sprained, but not broken," she said. "We need to splint it."

"We?" Wait. Would there be blood?! I can't stand the sight of blood. What color is flamingo blood, anyway? Pink?

Dr. Deerwin kept one hand resting gently on the bird while she pulled a drawer open with the other hand. She took out some foam pipe insulation, a couple of furniture hinges, and a roll of white surgical tape. This place was like a medical Home Depot.

"Don't just stand there!" (She meant me again.) "Tear me off a few lengths of tape—about five inches each."

I grabbed the roll of tape and started eyeballing five-inch strips as I tore them off. I stuck the strips on the edge of the table where Dr. Deerwin could reach them. She bound the flamingo's leg in pipe insulation and connected the upper and lower pieces of foam with the long, thin hinges. Then she wrapped the whole setup with surgical tape (provided by me).

"There. That should stabilize the ankle," she said. Ankle? It looked more like a knee to me, but what did I know about flamingo anatomy? I couldn't even identify the parts of a tadpole.

When the operation was finished, Dr. Deerwin lifted the flamingo off the table and lowered it slowly until its feet touched the floor. Then Penelope pulled the blanket away.

The flamingo flapped its wings. It looked wobbly and it was a little cranky, but when Dr. Deerwin let go, it stood up! Just like a lawn ornament! A little

lightbulb went on in my head. Maybe I'd do my report on *flamingos*!

Dr. Deerwin started to give Mr. Pincus a whole bunch of instructions. What kind of pen the flamingo needed. How much water. How often to feed it. What complications to watch for. Mr. Pincus grunted at the end, which I think meant *Got it*. When it came to animals (including birds), he was pretty much on the ball.

"I'll be back tomorrow to check on the leg," said Dr. Deerwin. As she was putting the extra tape and foam back in the drawer, she nodded to me.

"Good job," she said.

I don't know why it felt so special when she said that, but it did. This wasn't like "Good job" for building a spaghetti bridge or for loading the dishwasher the right way. It felt more important— like I'd really helped with something that mattered. An animal wasn't hurting anymore, and I'd played a (small) part in that.

"Thanks," I said. Mr. Pincus grunted.

I walked back to the Jeep with Penelope. I held the blanket, which was covered in soft pink feathers. Penelope carried the goggles. She was a little shorter than me, but she had a long stride. I hustled to keep up.

"So—you like animals?" I asked.

I know. Embarrassing. But that's the best I could think of. Penelope probably thought I was a total idiot. But she didn't show it, which made me like her right away.

"I d-d-do!" she said. "I've been around them m-my whole life." She took a flamingo feather from the blanket and stuck it into one of her braids. "But what I *really,* REALLY love—are b-b-b-*birds*!"

I scanned my past for a bird connection...wait... *got* one!

"My sister had a canary once," I said. I didn't want to tell her the whole story—about how Saffron got out of his cage and flew into the open freezer during a New Year's party when nobody was looking. I thought it might spoil the moment.

RIP Saffron

When we got to the Jeep, Penelope hopped into the backseat and strapped in. Dr. Deerwin came around the front and slid into the driver's seat. She started the engine and began to back out. Penelope leaned out the window.

"Hey!" she shouted. "If you really like b-b-birds, b-b-be here tomorrow. You haven't s-s-seen anything yet!"

CHAPTER 15

MUM'S THE WORD

Later that day. (Much later.)

Mom and Georgia were waiting for me outside the front gate. They'd been there for a while. Mom still wore her Swifty's waitress uniform. She was tapping on the steering wheel with her fingertips. Georgia sat in the backseat, counting the cash from her first week as a Math Mentor.

Junior sat next to her, nibbling a hole in one of my shoes. I opened the door and jumped into the front seat. Mom hit me with the classic *Rafe, you're late* look. It was all in the eyebrows. No words necessary. I knew that look all too well.

"Sorry," I said. "I had to help Mr. Pincus build a new pen." When I tugged on the seat belt strap, a pink feather floated out of my shirt collar.

"Rafe, I'm glad to see that you're working hard—but if something comes up, just call me, okay? I could have done another hour on my shift."

"Sorry, Mom. I will." Mom started the car up and pulled out onto the road toward home.

I felt bad. I knew how hard my mom worked. And I also knew that Swifty's Diner wasn't exactly her dream job. Mom is the artistic type too. In fact, what she really wanted to be was a painter. But I guess there aren't many painting jobs that pay enough to feed two kids. Especially when you're doing it on your own.

"Ten dollars, eleven dollars..." Georgia was counting out her money into neat little piles. I turned around and stared at her between the seats.

"Who do you think you are? Queen Midas?" I
said.

I should warn you that insulting Georgia
is usually a mistake because she has a way of
delivering the perfect comeback.

Sure enough: "Oh yeah?" she said. "What did
you make today?"

Told you. Low blow.

"Georgia!" said Mom. "Be nice!"

But actually, this time I had a comeback to *her*
comeback. I was about to say, "I made a *friend*. So

there!" But it sounded a little corny—even in my head. And besides, I knew Mom would ask way too many questions. So instead I said:

"Absolutely nothing."

Georgia seemed happy with that.

CHAPTER 16

RAPTOR RAPTURE

G-G-Get ready!"

It was the next morning. Just me and
Penelope in a far corner of the BushyTail property.
Nothing but an open field with a fence around it.
Penelope stood with her right arm extended all
the way out to her side. She wore a thick leather
glove with a cuff that went way up past her wrist.
Sitting on top of the glove was a strip of raw
chicken—like a Swifty's chicken tender before it
hit the fryer. All in all, it was a pretty weird setup.
But Penelope said I had to trust her. And for some
strange reason, I did.

I had no clue what was about to happen, and
I was a little nervous—especially after Penelope
told me to crouch down by her leg and not move a

muscle. My heart was thumping. I stared across the field. Nothing there.

And then I saw it. Heading straight for us.

At first it was just a small brown shape. It started low to the ground and then rose up.

What *was* it?

"Come on, sweetie!" Penelope whispered. (She didn't mean me.)

The shape got bigger and bigger, closer and closer—until it was almost on top of us. Right before it was about to crash into us, I couldn't help myself. I ducked and squeezed my eyes shut. I heard a *WHOMP!*

When I looked up, Penelope's glove had something attached to it. It was a freaking giant *owl*! It was about two feet tall and had yellowish-gold eyes, two feathery tufts sticking straight up from the top of its head, and a black beak. Each foot had four awesome talons that were latched on to Penelope's glove.

When Penelope said she had a surprise for me, she wasn't kidding. This was better than the opening of *Harry Potter*!

The owl stretched its wings out—wider than a closet door! It gobbled the chicken down in one gulp. Then it swiveled its head around and looked straight at me. I crouched down even lower. Was I about to get my eyes pecked out?

"D-D-Don't worry," said Penelope. "You're n-not on the m-menu!" She stroked the owl's head with two fingers of her other hand. The owl seemed to enjoy it.

"Does it have a name?" I asked.

"Her n-n-name is Lila," said Penelope. "She's a g-great horned owl. And she's my b-b-baby!"

First the flamingo save, and now *this*? Who *was* this girl? Some kind of bird whisperer? And where the heck do you pick up a great horned owl, anyway? I don't think they sell them down at PetSmart. That's when Penelope laid out the whole Lila tale for me. In a nutshell, this was it:

A few months ago, while Penelope was hiking in the woods, she found a bird nest on the ground. Inside was one tiny owlet. Guess who?

The mommy owl was nowhere around, and Penelope knew that a baby owl would be raccoon food that night for sure. So she brought the baby home in her pocket and made a nest in her barn. For one whole month, Penelope camped out there in a sleeping bag to keep the baby company. She fed her every day with an eyedropper.

When Lila's wings were strong enough, Penelope helped her learn how to *fly*! (It came pretty naturally, I guess.)

Then, over the next few months, she trained her to search for food.

"N-Now," said Penelope, "Lila can s-s-spot a piece of chicken from across a f-f-football field."

While I was taking all this in, Lila was standing patiently on Penelope's glove—digesting her food, I guess. Penelope looked over at me.

"W-W-Wanna hold her?" she asked.

What?? Who? Me? Now?? I was a little nervous. Scratch that. I was shaking like a leaf. But Penelope was looking at me and I didn't want to seem like a wimp.

"Sure. Why not?" I said, trying to sound cool and casual. I mean, nothing dangerous about handling a massive bird that has feet hooks designed for

shredding flesh, right? How do I get myself into
these situations?

Penelope handed me an extra glove. She had
come prepared. I slipped the long glove on and
wriggled my fingers a little to get the feel of it. It
was thick all over and padded on top. I felt like a
hockey goalie.

"Now hold your arm up," said Penelope, "and
stay very still." She didn't have to tell me twice.
At that point, I could have won the Mannequin
Challenge, no problem. The only thing moving
was my stomach—which was doing little flip-
flops. Penelope eased her glove right next to mine

until our thumbs touched. Lila shifted one foot onto my glove, then the other. And just like that, I was holding a great horned owl. I felt like the FalconMeister from Wormhole!

You'd think something built with so many feathers would be really light—but Lila felt like a family-size sack of rice. No wonder Penelope wanted a break.

Just as I was kind of getting used to having a huge bird of prey at my fingertips, Lila started moving. She lifted one hooked foot and then the other. Was she getting antsy? Did I do something wrong??

"Whasgoingon?" I asked. (I was trying not to move my lips.)

Now Lila was totally turned around and facing back in the direction she came from.

"R-Relax," said Penelope. "She's ready to f-f-fly."

"SowhadooIdoo?" I asked.

"On the c-c-count of three," said Penelope, "just l-l-lift your arm up—f-fast."

There was no way I felt qualified for owl launching. But I didn't have time to argue. The countdown had already started.

"One!"

I inhaled.

"T-T-Two!"

I closed my eyes.

"TH-THREE!"

I lifted my arm straight up. I felt a whoosh of air in my face. All of a sudden, my hand felt light as, well...a feather. And when I opened my eyes, Lila was already halfway across the field. Just a brown speck in the distance.

"Excellent t-takeoff!" said Penelope. "I th-think you have a f-flair for this!"

That was amazing! A little lightbulb went on in my head. Maybe I'd do my report on *owls*!

CHAPTER 17

MiRROR, MiRROR

O kay, so what's up with...?"

"Why is it that...?"

"How come you...?"

That was me, talking in front of the mirror in my bedroom, the night after my great owl adventure. I was practicing the question I wanted to ask Penelope, trying to come up with just the right words. And failing. Obviously.

If you've been paying attention to the story so far, you've probably noticed something about Penelope that makes her a little different. I mean, it's pretty obvious. And I'm not talking about her smarts, or her derring-do under pressure, or her magical abilities with anything that flies.

You know what it is. You're probably curious

too. So how would *you* ask about it, without getting too personal, or insulting her—or sounding like a complete jerk?

Don't look at me. I didn't have a clue.

CHAPTER 18

TALKING THE TALK

What a relief! I was off the hook! Penelope solved the problem!

She brought it up all by herself, the very next day. We were in the supply room at BushyTail, right next to the main office. She was helping me stock the refrigerator with frozen crickets.

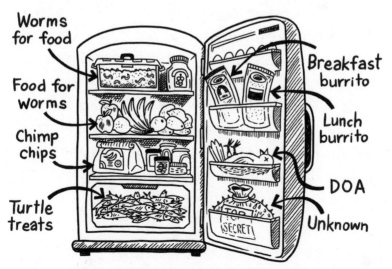

Worms for food

Food for worms

Chimp chips

Turtle treats

Breakfast burrito

Lunch burrito

DOA

Unknown

"In case you've been w-w-wondering," Penelope said, "I n-n-never s-stutter when I talk to animals. Only when I talk to p-p-people."

Okay, clearly this was a big moment. Penelope had just revealed something really personal about herself, and it probably wasn't easy for her. Somewhere in the depths of my mixed-up middle school brain, a voice cried out for a meaningful reply. Something sensitive and thoughtful. Instead, I blurted out the stupidest thing ever. "Maybe you were an animal in another life!"

I knew it was lame as soon as the words left my mouth. But Penelope was cool about it. She even laughed.

"I d-doubt it," she said. "I think it's that animals n-n-never judge or question." She passed me another bag of crickets. "D-Don't take how I t-talk p-personally, Rafe. I'm b-better with you than I am with m-most people. It's just a little quirk in my b-brain!"

I was really trying to get my head around this. I held up the bag of crickets. "So, you mean to tell me that if you talked to one of these crickets right now, you wouldn't stutter at all?"

Penelope plucked out a frozen cricket and put it in the palm of her hand. She took a breath and looked deep into its little compound eyes.

"Hi there," she said. "I'm Penelope. Sorry you're about to be lemur lunch."

Wow. I guess everybody's brain works in strange ways. Mine sure does. Anyway, I was glad to have that conversation behind me. It made me feel a little less awkward around Penelope. At least I knew where I stood with her—which was somewhere between most humans and a dead cricket.

For a Khatchadorian, that's progress!

CHAPTER 19

THINGS ARE LOOKING UP

Blaaarrrrt!

"Arf! Arf!"

I was riding in the golf cart with Mr. Pincus. Sulfur was sitting in the back. Every time the cart bounced, Mr. Pincus released a blast of burrito gas. Right on cue, Sulfur started barking. Not the most relaxing ride in the world. I was pretty excited, though (and a little nervous), because we were way off my usual route. Mr. Pincus was taking me to a part of the compound I had never even visited.

We left all the animals, birds, reptiles, and amphibians I knew in our rearview and headed off into unknown BushyTail territory. At least, unknown to me.

Pretty soon, the path wasn't even paved anymore. It was just a dirt trail—even bumpier than before. Which meant more burrito activity. Which meant more barking. It was a vicious circle. Or is it cycle? Either way, it was smelly and noisy.

Finally, we pulled up in front of a stockade fence—the wooden kind frontier folks built way back before fence-building companies were invented. The fence was really high. I probably couldn't have bounced to the top with a trampoline. And the logs were so close together it was impossible to see through.

Mr. Pincus hopped off the cart, pulled out a key, and unlocked a huge padlock on the fence. Then he pushed a heavy metal crossbar up and out of the way. He leaned his shoulder against the fence. A wide section swung open with a loud creak. I peeked inside.

What's behind door number one?

After three weeks at BushyTail, I thought I'd seen everything.

Wrong again.

Because standing in front of me—just a Frisbee toss away—were two huge giraffes! You heard me right. Actual, full-size, real-life *giraffes*! This was definitely *not* on the tour!

When you see giraffes in Google images, they're usually just standing around on the savannah. So it's hard to realize how tall they really are. In person, you wouldn't believe it! Think about it this way: According to the pencil marks Mom made on my bedroom door, I'm about four and a half feet tall (when I stand up straight). And from what I could see, four of me stacked up wouldn't even reach the top of a giraffe's head.

4 Rafes = 1 giraffe (almost)

Their necks seemed to go on forever. Their front legs were long and straight, with thick, knobby knees. Their back legs were a little shorter and bent in the middle. They were covered all over in brown rectangles with gold showing in between— like somebody painted patches on them from top to bottom with a big brush. They were like walking modern art! So totally cool!

When we came through the gate, the giraffes were busy nibbling leaves from a few tall bushes. But the branches were almost bare. Hardly enough for a decent brunch. The giraffes turned and looked right at us. They had stubby horns sticking straight up from their heads, like little furry antennas. And when they licked their lips, they had the world's longest tongues!

My tongue is almost as long as my neck!

"Ever seen an African giraffe?" asked Mr. Pincus. Last time I checked, there weren't many African giraffes roaming the streets of Hills Village.

"Only in *The Lion King*!" I said.

"Go get the alfalfa."

"The what?"

"In the bin."

I was a bit slow on the uptake, but now I realized why we towed a plastic box on wheels behind the golf cart. I'd figured it was extra burritos. I walked over, flipped the lid open, and saw that the bin was filled with thick green grass. It smelled like somebody just mowed a lawn in there. Giraffes must have a really good sense of smell because they started walking over right away.

They moved like they were in slow motion—so graceful and smooth. Quiet too. (Not that it's likely to happen, but a giraffe could definitely sneak up on you. So watch out.) Sulfur was running around like a lunatic, but he didn't seem to bother the giraffes one bit. From their eyeball level, he must have looked like a big yellow ant. Anyway, they were laser-focused on the alfalfa.

I grabbed as much as I could in my arms and carried it over to where Mr. Pincus was standing. He took a bunch of green leaves in one hand and held it out in front of him.

He grunted, meaning *Watch what I do.* He used that grunt a lot.

Now that the giraffes were closer, I could see that one was even taller than the other. And the shorter giraffe was a little plump in the rump.

"This is Cain," said Mr. Pincus as the tall giraffe dipped its head and nibbled alfalfa from his hand, "and that's Abel." I held out a bunch of alfalfa the same way. Abel took a big bunch and started chomping.

Cain and Abel. Where had I heard those names before? Oh, right—Grandma Dotty's bedtime Bible stories. Made sense. This whole place was kind of like a nutty Noah's Ark!

"Cain and Abel. So, they're brothers?" I asked.

"That's what I thought," said Mr. Pincus.

After I got more alfalfa, Mr. Pincus told me how it all went down:

A year ago, he got a call from a crazy Russian, who told him that a zoo in Omsk was going out of business—and there was a fire sale on giant mammals. The hippos were already taken. The warthogs were spoken for. But he still had a couple of giraffes to unload.

"Two boys. Good shape. No trouble," he said. (Imagine it with a thick Russian accent.)

I guess Mr. Pincus couldn't resist. He probably worried about the crazy Russian turning the giraffes loose out there in Siberia—where there are zero leaves to eat.

Anybody interested in matched set of *Giraffa Camelopardalis?* Fully housebroken!

The plump giraffe chomped another handful of alfalfa from my hand.

"Abel's got a big appetite!" I said. Mr. Pincus looked over at me.

"That's because she's eating for two," he said.

Hold on.

"She...? Eating for two?"

"The Russian lied," said Mr. Pincus. "These two aren't brothers. They're male and female. They're *mates*."

Did not see that coming. This was a world-class BushyTail twist!

Abel wasn't paunchy. She was pregnant!

CHAPTER 20

NEARING THE END

If you're eating a snack right now, you might want to put it down. Because you're not going to believe what happened a couple of days later.

I was back in the giraffe stockade. This time I was with Dr. Deerwin and Penelope. We rode up in the Jeep, which was a lot smoother than the golf cart—even though I always get a little barf-ish when I ride in the backseat.

I'd never thought about it, but I guess pregnant animals need regular checkups, just like pregnant people. And that's what Dr. Deerwin was there for. But I didn't know exactly what she had in mind.

First, she gave Abel some alfalfa. Then she ran her hands all along her sides and the back of her haunches (that's the animal word for *butt*). Abel seemed really relaxed and peaceful. I guess she didn't know what was coming any more than I did.

"Penelope, get my bag, please," said Dr. Deerwin.

"You b-b-bet!" said Penelope. She zipped off to the Jeep and came back with a black case the size of a small carry-on. Meanwhile, Dr. Deerwin unfolded a metal stepladder and set it up alongside one of Abel's back legs. She reached into the bag and pulled out the biggest thermometer I'd ever seen. Then she pointed to the stepladder.

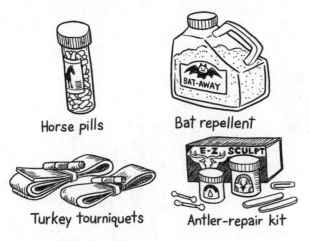

Horse pills

Bat repellent

Turkey tourniquets

Antler-repair kit

"Okay, Rafe," said Dr. Deerwin. "Up you go. I need you to hold Abel's tail out of the way."

Was this a job I really wanted? I thought about trying to worm out of it, but Penelope was watching. "Show no fear," I said to myself. I climbed up to the fourth step. My head was about level with the lower part of Abel's back. I grabbed her tail, which had a long black tuft at the end. It felt like a warm rope.

"Higher," said Dr. Deerwin. I lifted the tail a few more inches.

That's when it happened. Dr. Deerwin took the business end of the big thermometer and stuck it right into Abel's...I can't say it, but I can show you a picture...

Abel didn't even blink. I'm pretty sure I would have jumped about a mile.

A few seconds later, the thermometer gave a couple of quick beeps. Dr. Deerwin pulled it out and read the digits.

"One oh two point five!" she called.

"One oh t-t-two p-point five!" Penelope repeated, writing the number down in a large notebook. "G-Got it!"

"All's well in babyland," said Dr. Deerwin.

If you'd told me on the last day of school that I'd be getting this personal with an animal the size of a two-story building, I would have said, "You're crazy!" But I really loved the giraffes—and I couldn't *wait* for Abel to have her baby. In fact, I pretty much loved *all* the critters at BushyTail. Even the weird ones. I was starting to feel like I'd finally found a job I was kind of good at. And that was a pretty great feeling.

Too bad it didn't last.

"Rafe Khatchadorian!!!"

I dropped Abel's tail and almost fell off the ladder.

I knew from years of life experience that when somebody called me by my first and last name, it always meant trouble—whether the name-caller was Mom, Grandma Dotty, or Principal Stricker. This time, it was Mr. Pincus.

He was in the golf cart, driving even crazier than usual. When he stopped, he nearly flew over the front end. His shirt was sweaty and his face was red, kind of like he was about to have a heart attack. I wondered if Dr. Deerwin had anything in her bag for that.

Mr. Pincus looked straight at me.

"Rafe! Did you feed the lemurs this morning?"

Of course I did. It was my favorite thing to do. I nodded.

"Do you happen to remember locking the gate?"

I got a funny little sting in my gut. *Think, Rafe, think!* I remembered being inside with the lemurs. I remembered Dr. Deerwin pulling up in the Jeep. I remembered being happy to see her—and even happier to see Penelope. I remembered putting down the cricket pail and waving. I remembered heading out the gate of the lemur enclosure toward the Jeep. But that's where my memory stopped.

Not good, Rafe. Not good at *all*!

CHAPTER 21

CUT TO THE CHASE!

Know what a group of lemurs is called? You won't believe it. A *conspiracy*. That's right. A conspiracy of lemurs. And that's exactly what this felt like. All ten lemurs had *conspired* against me to escape!

Okay, I might have left the gate unlatched. My bad, no question. But that didn't mean they had to go rogue! They could have just romped around on their jungle gym until I got back. They probably could have even locked the gate themselves with their little paw-hands if they wanted to.

Instead, they were making me look really bad. Keeping the animals safe and secure was Job #1 at BushyTail. And I'd botched it. To make it worse, finding ten lemurs in this crazy maze was going to be almost impossible.

Lemurs are really fast. They can leap and swing and climb like nobody's business. And when they hold still, they can be almost invisible, like little gray ghosts. And it wasn't like we could call out a big search party like in the movies. The search party was *us*!

Dr. Deerwin and Penelope and I piled into the Jeep. We followed Mr. Pincus back to the lemur enclosure (the scene of the crime). Sure enough, the gate was wide open and the place was empty. Not even a good-bye note!

Fortunately for me, Dr. Deerwin seemed to have a plan—and she had the equipment to go with it. She dug around in the back of the Jeep and screwed together a long metal pole with a lasso at the end of it. Penelope pulled out a big net and strapped on an industrial-strength head lamp. It looked like she was going mining for butterflies. She handed another net to me, while Dr. Deerwin tested the lasso on a metal post. Worked great. But of course, the post wasn't bouncing around like a lemur that had just tasted freedom. Good luck with that.

"Now listen," said Dr. Deerwin. "They probably scattered. No way we're going to find all ten of them in one place. We need to split up too."

Dr. Deerwin sent Mr. Pincus off down the path toward the frog lagoon in the golf cart. He floored it.

"Slow down, Mr. Pincus!" she shouted after him. "You'll scare them away!"

Mr. Pincus eased off on the pedal. A little.

"Rafe," said Dr. Deerwin, "you know this place better than we do. Any ideas?"

I tried to put my guilty feelings on pause and switch on what was left of my brain. If I were a lemur, where would I go?

"Well, there's a grove of trees down past the skunk hut. That's good climbing territory."

"Okay," Dr. Deerwin said, "I'll go in that direction. Penelope, you check the perimeter. If they get over that outer fence, they're gone for good."

I felt my heart sink. Along with my stomach.

"O-k-kay!" said Penelope. She put the pole of her net over her shoulder and took off. Dr. Deerwin turned to me.

"Rafe, you check around all the buildings by the entrance. Look on the roofs, windowsills, any little corners where they might be hiding. And watch for open windows!"

I was kind of hoping Dr. Deerwin would let me

and Penelope search as a team. A little company would have been nice. Now I was just lost in my own sorry thoughts.

I watched Dr. Deerwin and Penelope disappear in opposite directions. Then I started walking down the twisty path that led to the main entrance.

"C'mon, guys! Give me a break!" I was talking to myself as I walked, but also to the lemurs, just in case they could hear me. Maybe they'd recognize my voice, run out of the bushes, and start climbing all over me for old times' sake. But after a while with no sign of a lemur, I realized it was no use.

To catch a lemur, you have to *think* like one.

CHAPTER 22

WHAT GOES UP...

Back near the main entrance, a little way from the office, there was a huge tree. A weeping willow, Mr. Pincus told me on my first day. Pretty appropriate for the way I felt at the moment. The tree was older than BushyTail—maybe even older than Mr. Pincus! It had a thick trunk and branches with long, stringy green leaves that drooped toward the ground. The tree gave me an idea. Why not get a top-down view of my surroundings? Couldn't hurt. At least, that's what I thought.

When it came to climbing, my skills were a little rusty. I was no lemur, let's put it that way. I skinned my elbow on the first branch and scraped my knee on some rough bark a little higher up. But before I knew it, I was about twenty feet off the ground. Giraffe height! My arms were wrapped around the trunk of the tree and my feet were wedged into a little *V* where a couple of branches went their separate ways. From way up there, I could see the main office building, the clinic, and a couple of small sheds where we stored tools and tarps and stuff. There was also a little fenced-in area where we kept the garbage cans.

Rafe's-eye view

When I looked behind me, I saw Eight Ball the turtle in his pool, still swimming in circles. I heard pigs snorting and wildebeests huffing and howler monkeys howling. Way off in the distance past the gate, I saw cars zooming along the main road. I hoped lemurs didn't know how to hitchhike.

I scanned the whole area, just like Dr. Deerwin said, trying not to miss any details. I saw chipmunks. I saw squirrels. But nothing with a ringed tail. I'll bet Lila could have spotted a lemur from a mile away. But not me. Not with my ordinary eyes, which felt like they were about to pop out of my head from staring.

Coming from way back in the compound, I heard the chimps chattering and screeching. I think they knew what was going on. They were probably having a good laugh at my expense. Rafe-shaming was their specialty!

DRIP! DRIP!

What now?

As if my luck couldn't get any worse, it was starting to rain! Great. I felt the first few warm drops on my neck and head, then turned up my shirt collar. This was going to make the search even harder! I looked up through the branches. Not a cloud in the sky. Weird. I rubbed my fingers across my wet neck. Wait. That smell! I'd know it anywhere! And at that moment, it was the most delightful fragrance in the world.

Lemur pee!

I looked up again. Sure enough, I caught a glimpse of a small black-and-white tail poking through a bunch of green willow leaves! I climbed up a few more feet. The tail disappeared. Typical lemur evasive maneuver. I moved farther out on the branch. Suddenly a furry little head popped out through the leaves in front of me. It was one of the lemur babies! Leon? Larry? I could never keep the names straight.

"Hold still, little guy! I got you!" I [...] calm instead of annoyed (which is what [...] was). I noticed that Dr. Deerwin and Pene[...] always used a soft, reassuring voice when th[...] talked to animals, so I tried to follow their exam[...]

"C'mon, little fella! Come to Uncle Rafe!" But [...] the lemur wasn't having any of it. Instead of coming closer, he started backing up—out toward the skinny end of the branch!

I figured I had one chance to make a grab, so I went for it. I hooked my legs around the branch, like riding a very skinny horse. I shimmied forward. The little lemur was about three feet away. But I could tell from the baby's body language that he was getting ready to do a classic lemur leap. After that, I knew all bets would be off.

I kept one arm around the branch and stretched waayyy out with the other hand, feeling for anything furry. And then...

CRRRRRACCCK!

You know that sound, right?

It's the sound of a branch snapping.

My branch.

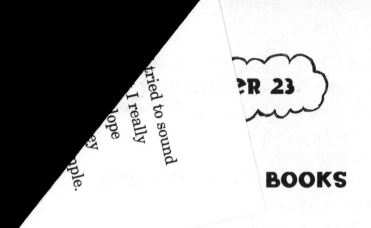

tried to sound
I really
lope
ey
ple.

BOOKS

Rafe! What h-h-happened t-to you?!"
       I was half-walking, half-limping back up
the path toward the lemur enclosure, wheeling
a large garbage can in front of me. Penelope ran
over, looking really worried. It was probably the
purple lump on my head that got her attention.
My other big sore spot was on my rear end—but
nobody was going to be seeing *that* bruise anytime
soon.

       "I'm fine," I said. "Really. Just a little tree
tumble."

Note: If you absolutely have to fall out of a tree, a weeping willow isn't a bad choice. The branches were kind of springy, so I sort of bounced my way down.

The baby lemur landed on top of me and tried to make a run for it. When I cornered him in the garbage hutch, he hopped inside one of the empty cans. I closed the lid. Gotcha! I could hear him banging around inside the can all the way back. Don't do the crime if you can't do the time, my friend!

I saw Dr. Deerwin looking through the fence around the lemur enclosure, her lasso pole resting on the ground. When I got closer, my heart started to do a little happy dance. Because—miracle of miracles—the enclosure was crawling with lemurs!

"You found them?!" I said to Dr. Deerwin. I wanted to hug her!

"Oh, I got a few," said Dr. Deerwin. "But actually, Penelope's the star. She found most of them all on her own."

"Guess I've g-got a g-good lemur d-detector," said Penelope. I could tell that Dr. Deerwin was really proud of her. And I could tell that Penelope was really proud to be somebody her mom was really proud of. Which only made me feel like more of a loser. Not that it was a competition or anything, but I definitely felt like the weakest link, search-wise.

"Well, at least I found *one*!" I said.

I wheeled the garbage can into the enclosure and popped the lid off. The baby lemur jumped out like he was shot from a cannon and ran off to join his buddies.

"Six...seven..."

Mr. Pincus stood in the middle of the enclosure doing a head count.

"...Eight...NINE!"

He counted again. Same result.

Only nine? Are you kidding me?

"It's Loretta!" said Mr. Pincus. "We're still missing Loretta!" (How the heck did he tell them apart?)

Penelope grabbed the lasso pole and tugged at my sleeve.

"C'mon!" she said. "We g-g-got this!"

She started down the path—back in the direction I just came from. As usual, I had to hustle to keep up with her. Penelope had energy to spare, even after tracking down a bunch of desperate fugitives.

"Where are we going?" I asked.

"You f-found the b-b-baby back by the office, right?"

I nodded.

"Well, his m-mom is p-probably there too!"

"Hey, Rafe!" called Dr. Deerwin. "No trees, please!"

My left butt cheek twinged a little with every step. But I felt like I was with a real lemur-catching expert now. If anybody could save the day, Penelope could!

When we got to the main buildings, we looked in every garbage can, under every piece of wood, behind every bush, in every dark corner.

No stone unturned.

Then, just as we were passing the office again, I heard a noise from inside. Like somebody tearing paper.

"Penelope!" I whisper-yelled. I pointed toward the window, which I noticed was open just a crack. You know what they say: "Give a lemur an inch..."

Penelope moved underneath the window and tipped her ear up, listening. She nodded.

We moved around to the front door and opened it—verrrrry slowly. We tiptoed inside. I had my net ready. Penelope had her pole. The office was dark, so Penelope switched on her head lamp. The light beam bounced all around the room and then pointed up at the bookshelf where the sound was coming from.

Suddenly we saw two round eyes reflecting back at us.

It was Loretta, all right! And she wasn't just sitting there. She was chewing her way through the entire BushyTail animal library! There were little scraps of paper everywhere, like lemur-made confetti. A couple of gnawed-up books had already dropped onto the desk. Loretta had eaten through half of *Watership Down* and most of *The Feeding Habits of African Ruminants*. Now she was working on the cover of *Old Yeller*—the collectors' edition. All that was left was *Old Yell...* Mr. Pincus was going to be so mad!

"Okay, Loretta," said Penelope softly. "Time to go home, Mama..."

She stretched out the long pole until the lasso was about an inch away from Loretta's head. *Nice try, human,* Loretta seemed to say! She jumped from the shelf onto a lamp that hung from the ceiling on a long white cord. She stood up on the lampshade, wrapped her paws around the cord, and started swinging like a trapeze artist—just like on the ropes back at the jungle gym.

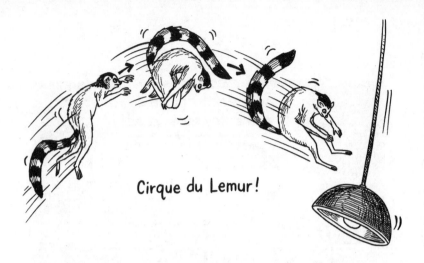

Cirque du Lemur!

That gave me an idea! I looked at Penelope. "Wait!" I said. "Don't move!"

I backed slowly out of the door and then ran around, going in the rear entrance of the storage room. I opened the refrigerator and grabbed a bunch of crickets! Then I ran back into the office. Loretta was still swinging on the lamp. At this point, I felt like she was rubbing it in my face a little bit. Taunting me for my mistake. Daring me to make a move.

Well, I was done playing fair.

I held out the crickets.

Loretta looked down. Her eyes got even wider. Her little wet nose sniffed. Her pointy ears twitched. She dropped from the lamp, did

a catapult off the copy machine, landed on my
shoulder, and plopped right into my arms.

I could tell that Penelope was impressed.

"N-N-Nice catch!" she said. I had to admit, it was pretty slick.

But was it too little too late?

CHAPTER 24

DOWN AND OUT

Just as I expected, the next morning was Judgment Day.

I sat across from Mr. Pincus in his lemur-trashed office. It looked like a kids' birthday party gone wrong. There were tiny chewed-up bits of paper all over the floor, all over the shelves, all over the desk. There was even a hole in Mr. Pincus's spare straw hat.

When Penelope and I had brought Loretta back the afternoon before, Mr. Pincus hadn't said much. I apologized every which way about leaving that gate open. And I really, really meant it! But from the way Mr. Pincus was grunting now, I kind of knew how much trouble I was in.

"Rafe," he said, "you're a good kid…"

I knew there was a "but" coming.

"But…I think you might be a little too absent-minded for animal work."

I slumped in the chair. I've had a lot of bad moments in my life, but this one was in the Hall of Shame. In fact, it might have been the worst. Not just because I messed up. Nothing new there. It was because I messed up at something I really, really loved.

"You're firing me?" I said.

"Well, technically, I can't really fire a volunteer," he said. "I'm offering you a transfer."

A transfer? Like a *school* transfer? I thought Mr. Pincus might be sending me back to Hills Village summer school. Suddenly I had visions of tadpoles swimming in my head.

But I underestimated Mr. Pincus. He had something totally different up his sleeve.

CHAPTER 25

STARTING OVER, ALL OVER AGAIN

I had to call Mom to come pick me up early. When I got in the car, I told her the story about the end of my BushyTail career and about my new "opportunity," as Mr. Pincus put it. I talked fast, trying not to look at Mom's disappointed face.

The "opportunity" was this: Mr. Pincus had a brother who ran a fancy resort in the Gunkledunk Mountains. A real high-end place, he said. One of the kids on the staff just came down with Rocky Mountain spotted fever (the Gunkledunk variety), and Mr. Pincus's brother needed a replacement through the end of the summer.

Mr. Pincus gave me a recommendation letter (sort of). It said, "Bright. Works hard. Keep him away from animals." I guess under the circumstances, two out of three wasn't bad.

I could tell Mom was upset, and I couldn't really blame her.

"Rafe, this is crazy!" she said. "The Gunkledunks are four hours away!"

"Sorry, Mom," I said. And I really was. I was also pretty mad—but mostly at myself. I knew how big my mistake was. The lemurs could have gotten lost or hurt. And then I would have felt even *more* terrible.

I kind of wanted Mom to yell at me—to get it out of her system and clear the air. But she just got kind of quiet. She took a deep breath. I could see her Mom-mind working. She looked straight ahead through the car windshield. After she calmed down a little, she reached over and put her hand on my shoulder.

"Look. I'll call Mr. Pincus tomorrow and see what the deal is with his brother's place," she said. "But I'll be honest, Rafe, I don't know how we're going to work this out."

I didn't say anything for the whole ride home. I had that burning little lump in my throat, like when you kind of want to cry but you're too embarrassed to let it out.

How Low Rafe Feels

Lower than a boa constrictor's belly

Lower than a dung beetle's dinner.

Lower than a centipede's shoelaces

Because I knew I'd let everybody down. And I'd never get to see the baby giraffe being born. And I didn't get a chance to say good-bye to Penelope.

And...I never even *started* my animal report!

CHAPTER 26

THREE FOR THE ROAD!

Georgia counted out crisp dollar bills onto the table at Swifty's Diner, lining them up so all the faces pointed the same way. I had to admit—it was a pretty impressive pile of presidents.

"Not a bad month!" she said. "Some of the parents even gave me tips!"

As for me, I just sat there sipping my second jumbo Zoom soda, wondering why I couldn't do anything right. For the last week, while my sister raked in the green for her final Math Mentor sessions, I'd been sitting around the house, playing TrollQuest in solo mode. But my heart wasn't in it. I could hardly make it past level one. All of my gaming skills were gone—and so was my confidence. Let's face it: I had flamed out as a

BushyTail Volunteer. And all the troll treasure in the world couldn't make up for it.

While I was busy sulking, Mom had a few talks with Mr. Pincus about this plan to have me work at his brother's resort. And finally—unbelievably—it all got arranged! The summer was kind of slow at Swifty's, which meant Mom could actually take some time off. Georgia was done with her tutoring. So we decided to make it a family adventure. Grandma Dotty would hold down the fort back home. (She said she wasn't about to give up her

bingo nights "for some crazy trip to the sticks.")
Junior would stay behind to keep her company.
There were plenty of raccoons to chase in Hills
Village. He didn't need a whole forest full of them.
It sounded like a good plan. Georgia and Mom
would chill out in nature while I was working.
Mom said she might try to do a little painting. Mr.
Pincus told us his brother even had a cabin on the
property where we could stay for free.

"Until Rafe burns it down," said Georgia. I
guess I deserved that.

Anyway, today was the day. We were ready to
head out at the end of Mom's morning shift. The
Khatchadorianmobile sat outside at the curb, all
gassed up and ready to roll. At 12:01 on the dot, Mom
walked out of the back of the diner with her cheeriest
face. She'd done a quick change from her waitress
uniform into jeans and a Hills Village Yoga T-shirt.
She already had a relaxation vibe from head to toe.

Swifty himself gave us a little wave from
behind the counter—like a blessing from the Pope.

"Ready, guys?" said Mom. "Let's make the most
of this. I hear the Gunkledunks are beautiful this
time of year!"

Georgia stacked up her bills into one huge pile. "Can we stop at the bank first?" she asked. "I want to deposit my cash before somebody thinks about stealing it." She was looking at me.

Way to rub it in, Miss Moneybags.

After a quick detour to the Hills Village Bank & Trust, we headed out of town, taking the Elm Street route past my school. Pretty soon, we were on the highway headed north. A few minutes later, we passed the turnoff to BushyTail. I got a little *ping* in my belly as the sign went by, but I had to let it go. Been there. Done that. Screwed it up. As usual.

I don't know about you, but the only way I can keep from barfing while I'm riding in the backseat is to keep my window open and lean out. Resting my chin on the window ledge, I felt the breeze in my hair. I held my palm up and let it catch air, which made it feel like a wing, which reminded me of Lila the owl, which reminded me of Penelope, which reminded me of the runaway lemurs, which reminded me of why I was in this situation in the first place. As if I needed reminding.

Georgia was wearing her earbuds and belting out "Never Enough" from *The Greatest Showman*. Never enough. Was she taking a dig at me—or was I being too sensitive? Her voice was so loud that even my noise-canceling headphones couldn't cancel her out.

I stuck my head farther out the window to taste the wind—and immediately sucked in a giant bug. Cough! Gag! Choke! Gross!

Probably an omen.

CHAPTER 27

CReAM OF THe CAMPS

Four hours and two Zoom-related rest stops later, we were deep in Gunkledunk territory. And Mom was right, the mountains *were* beautiful. Lots of green trees and shiny streams and smooth blue lakes. Like I said before, I'm more of an inside kid, but I had to admit that the great outdoors could be pretty impressive. Well done, Mother Nature!

The nice scenery helped distract me from my worries—kind of. For Mom and Georgia, this was time off without a care in the world. For me, it was another chance to prove myself. Or fail miserably. And my track record wasn't great.

When the road got steeper and the pavement got rougher, I started to worry that our car wouldn't make it. Whining sounds came from under the hood and some weird banging from underneath my seat. Mom kept two hands tight on the steering wheel and did her best to dodge the holes in the road. After another mile or so, the GPS said to turn left. So we did.

All of a sudden, the road evened out into a nice bed of gravel. It crunched under the tires like popcorn. The road curved around through green hills and tall trees for a mile or so until we came to a huge metal gate with a sign. It said WELCOME TO GREEN BANKS RESORT.

Green Banks! We had arrived! This was the place! I couldn't see any of the resort yet, but the sign looked pretty expensive. It was one of those big hand-carved models, with shiny gold lettering. Top-notch.

In front of the gate, there was a little speaker on a metal pole. As soon as we stopped, it spoke.

"May I help you?" Even the speaker voice sounded ritzy.

Mom leaned out of her window like she was ordering burgers at a drive-thru. "We're the Khatchadorians," she said. "Mr. Pincus is expecting us!"

"Stand by, please," said the voice. This was like gaining entry to some kind of super-secret spy complex. I wondered if they'd check our fingerprints. Or our eyeballs. I looked around for hidden cameras. (Probably disguised as pinecones.)

Mostly, I was praying our car wouldn't give up and die at the entrance. That would have been totally embarrassing.

The voice came back. "Proceed," it said. I heard a low hum. The gates opened. Mom drove through.

My first impression: this was *nothing* like Camp Wannamorra! There were paved trails and cabins nestled among the trees—except that they weren't really cabins. They were more like luxury cottages. I saw two guys playing golf on a putting green in the middle of the woods, like somebody had rolled out a smooth green carpet right over the roots and leaves.

When we passed a cottage close to the road, I saw a family unloading their suitcases from the back of their Grand Rover. Their luggage was probably worth more than our whole car.

There goes the neighborhood!

Mom's eyes were as big as two Swifty pies, and Georgia just kept saying "Wow!" over and over. I wanted to be excited too, but to be honest, I was getting a little nervous. Did I really belong here? At BushyTail, with a bunch of misfit animals, I kind of fit in.

But from the way it looked, Green Banks might be way out of my league.

HiGH EXPECTATiONS

Rafe, I've heard a lot about you!"

I was sitting across the desk from Sheldon Pincus, who was pretty much a Xerox copy of his brother, except that he had a woodsy lumberjack beard. I wondered if he liked burritos too. If I had to guess, he looked like more of a pancake type of guy. His office was my first stop. Mom and Georgia explored outside while Mr. Pincus and I had a get-acquainted chat.

It was funny how much the Pincus brothers' offices looked alike. Lots of clutter. Lots of bug spray. And loads of books. Obviously, they both loved to read, but instead of animal books, *this* Mr. Pincus was into *Edible Berries of the Gunkledunks,* *Knots for Knotheads,* and *Cooking for Billionaires.*

I guess to run a resort this fancy, you had to be a jack-of-all-trades.

"So. Rafe. My brother explained everything," said Mr. Pincus. "And I want you to think of this as a brand-new start. We've got plenty here at Green Banks to keep you busy. And don't worry—nothing involving animals!"

I had to admit I was kind of relieved about that. I felt like I'd done enough damage for one summer, and I sure didn't want to be responsible for any more wildlife disasters! Mr. Pincus (the farty one) hadn't said much about Green Banks except that it was a summer hideaway for people with lots of money. He was pretty vague about what I'd be doing. So this seemed the right time to ask.

"Mr. Pincus, can you tell me what my job will be, exactly?"

"Job?" said Mr. Pincus. "Rafe, it's not just *one* job. It's *every* job! It's whatever needs to be done! What you'll be doing depends on the day. But I promise you won't get bored!"

The door opened behind me. I heard heavy boots clomping.

"Ah, Gavin! Just in time!" said Mr. Pincus.

"Rafe, meet your supervisor, Gavin Groose!"

I turned around and looked up. And up. Gavin was a teenager, probably just a few years older than me. But he was one of those teenagers who already looked like a grown-up—tall and thick, with the beginning of a belly. The goatee added a few years, for sure. He wore a green T-shirt that said STAFF SUPERVISOR on the front. He should have asked for a larger size because he was bursting out of it in every direction. Gavin was bigger than Miller the Killer—and he looked even meaner. His mouth had a built-in sneer, so even his smile looked a little evil!

"Welcome to Green Banks," said Gavin with a sneer-smile. I stood up. We shook hands. It felt like being gripped in a vise from the Hills Village tool shop. I think Gavin kind of enjoyed it.

Mr. Pincus stood up behind his desk and rubbed his hands together. "First things first," he said. "Let's get you and the ladies squared away in your cabin!"

"I'll lead the way," said Gavin. He clomped over to the door and held it open. It was probably the last nice thing he ever did for me.

Mom and Georgia were just back from their stroll as we came out. Gavin barely gave them a glance.

"Follow me!" he said. Mom, Georgia, and I piled back into the car. Gavin hopped on a tricked-out PowerQuad ATV and revved the engine a few times, just to show off. Then he did a doughnut in the driveway and headed off down a wide trail.

"Who's the jerk?" asked Georgia.

"My supervisor," I said.

"You're working for Frankenstein?"

"Georgia! Manners!" said Mom. "We're guests here!"

Mom was right. All things considered, I guess we *were* kind of lucky. So what if I was getting paid less than Georgia got for being a Math Mentor. So what if my supervisor seemed like a total psycho. We were out in nature and we were surrounded by luxury. And we were staying for *nothing*.

As Mom followed Gavin out of the parking lot, I started imagining what our cabin would be like. Based on everything we'd seen on the way in, I had high hopes.

The work might be hard, but at least I'd be living like a king, right?

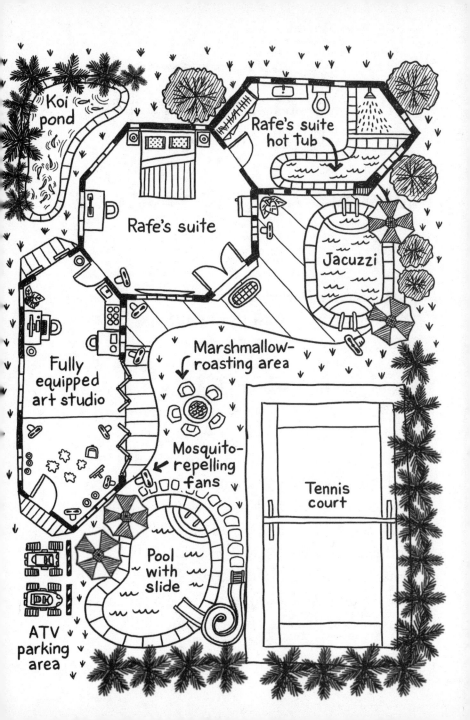

CHAPTER 29

THE BIG AND THE SMALL OF IT

As Mom followed Gavin, I tried to get the lay of the land. BushyTail was huge, but this place was even huger! And every building I saw screamed "Money!" at the top of its lungs. We drove past the Green Banks Dining Hall. It was made of stone, with thick wooden doors and a huge chimney. It looked like a really cool medieval castle. Then we passed the Green Banks Rec Center, which had an outdoor ropes course, a zip line, and a setup for trapeze classes—complete with a net. Through the trees, we could see sailboats rocking at the Green Banks Marina. And outside the Green Banks Arts Center, a bunch of kids played violins on the lawn. I mean, really played. Not like the Hills Village Middle School

Quartet, which sounded like four cats dying. This place was amazing!

Pretty soon, the trail began to narrow. The ride got so bumpy that Georgia started turning green. I stuck my head out the window for air and got whacked by a vine. Gavin sped ahead of us like a wild man, bouncing over ruts in the road and daring us to keep up with him. Maybe he didn't know our car was on its last legs. More likely he didn't care.

And then...straight ahead at the end of the trail...there it was! Our home in the wilderness!

Ready?

If this book were an animated movie, you'd be hearing the sad trombone sound right now. Because what we were looking at wasn't a cabin/cottage at all. It was more of a cottage/shack.

Welcome
~~Catchidurians~~
~~Kitchidubians~~
Khatchadorians!

Mom stopped the car in front of the place. Georgia opened her door and just stared.

"OMG. What do they think we are—*hobbits*?" she said.

"I think it's kind of cute!" said Mom. Leave it to Jules Khatchadorian to always look on the bright side. One of the many reasons I love her.

Gavin did a crazy spin-turn on his ATV and pulled up to the car. He handed Mom the key to the cottage and stared down at me with beady black eyes.

"Work starts at eight a.m. sharp. Main office. See you then, Lemur Lad!" Gavin laughed like a movie villain and zipped off, spraying dirt and pebbles onto the side of our car.

"Lemur Lad?" I guess Gavin knew all about my BushyTail mishap. So it looked like my new job came with a new nickname. Great.

Georgia and Mom were already on the front porch of the hobbit hut, all itchy to go inside. Mom stuck the key in the door and opened it. I hopped out of the car and joined them for a tour of our new digs. It was a very short tour.

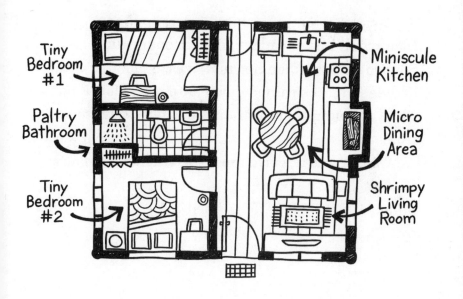

Tiny Bedroom #1

Paltry Bathroom

Tiny Bedroom #2

Miniscule Kitchen

Micro Dining Area

Shrimpy Living Room

If you're looking for Bedroom #3, you can stop looking. Because there wasn't one. I could NOT believe it! I traveled four hours and hundreds of miles to share a bedroom with my kid *sister*? In bunk beds, no less??

Think small!

"I call top bunk!" shouted Georgia. She scampered up the ladder like a monkey and flopped backward on her mattress. A cloud of dust and dead moths rained down onto my pillow. And I had a feeling there were more where they came from.

Welcome to Green Banks—Khatchadorian Sector.

CHAPTER 30

MUDDLE IN THE PUDDLE

Grandma Dotty always says, *You never get a second chance to make a first impression.* So I decided to get an early start on my first day of work. Georgia was still asleep when I got up. In the bedroom closet, I found a folded pair of shorts in my size, along with a green T-shirt that said STAFF across the chest—and across the back too. I guess that was in case they found me facedown in a lake or something.

Mom fixed me some scrambled eggs and I slurped down some OJ. Then I tucked in my T-shirt and finger-combed my hair.

"Now, Rafe," Mom said, "it's a new day. Remember to keep your head up and your eyes open—and do your best!"

"I will, Mom," I said. And I really, truly meant it. I wasn't about to let her down again. Not if I could help it.

After a classic Mom good-luck hug, I headed off down the path toward the main office. It was one of those mornings where the sun comes through the trees like light from heaven. All around me, birds were doing their cheerful chirping. The air was cool and it smelled like Christmas trees. The whole scene made me feel kind of optimistic.

That didn't last long.

I was about halfway down the paved part of the trail when I spotted two kids about my age coming toward me from the other direction. But they weren't walking. They were *floating*! Was it an optical illusion, or did they possess some kind of Green Banks superpowers? When they got closer, I saw that they were riding on hoverboards. And not the kind you buy at a yard sale. These were super-rad SyncroMax Hyperdrive X-50s— the kind I could only drool over. I tried not to drool.

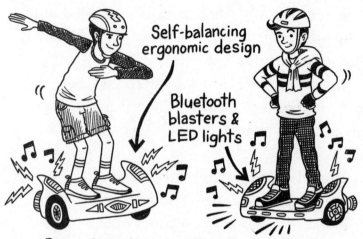

Self-balancing ergonomic design

Bluetooth blasters & LED lights

Price: If you have to ask, you can't afford it!

I could tell right away that these kids were guests, not staff. And when they got even closer, I could even see their names sewn in fancy writing on the pockets of their Green Banks polo shirts. So classy. The first guy was Skip. The other guy was Kai. As soon as they spotted me, they started weaving back and forth, acting all cool and stuff. Pretty soon, they were hovering right in front of me. Kai tried to show off with a one-foot roundabout. But he didn't have the skills—not even close. His board shot out from under him and flew into a huge mud puddle. It landed in the muck with a big, juicy *gloop!* Epic fail. Shameful. I didn't know what to say.

"Hey, greengrub!" Kai was talking to me. Terrific. *Another* nickname. "Can't you see I lost my board?" He pointed toward the puddle. "Go fetch!"

I felt like saying "Fetch it yourself, Richie Rich!" But I could hear Grandma's voice buzzing in my ear: *You never get a second chance to make a first impression!* And I'd run out of chances to screw up, so I pasted on a big smile.

"No problem," I said. "Piece of cake!"

I tiptoed to the edge of the puddle, trying not to get my white sneakers dirty. I stretched out over the murky muck, reaching my fingers as far as they would go. Almost! Just one more inch! I touched the front tip of the board. Got it!

Then…WHOOPSIE! I lost my balance and flopped facedown into the puddle, which made an even *bigger gloop!*

I guess Skip and Kai thought it was the funniest thing they'd seen all morning. They

laughed so loud it scared the birds off. I tried to
think of a way to preserve my dignity, but who
was I kidding? I had no dignity left. I grabbed the
board and pulled it out of the mud. Then I stood up
and handed it over.

Kai stopped laughing just long enough to say,
"Nice form, greengrub!" Then he started laughing
all over again. Skip and Kai hovered up the trail
past me, laughing all the way. No doubt they'd be
telling this story around the campfire tonight.

I tried to wipe the mud off the front of my T-shirt. No use. I only made it worse. Then I felt something squirmy and ticklish in my front pocket. I peeked in and saw a couple of tadpoles. It was like a message from Manta, reminding me I *still* hadn't started my animal report.

CHAPTER 31

JUST SCRAPING BY

So much for being early my first day. By the time I got to the office, Gavin was already there, tapping his foot and looking annoyed. As I walked up, he bent his big, hairy arm to check his Woodsman Explorer watch.

"Lemur Lad! You're *late*!" He looked me up and down and gave me a full-on smile-sneer. "And you're a *mess*! Not up to Green Banks standards! Didn't you read the manual?"

Actually, I tried, but there were so many rules, it put me to sleep. I started to tell him about Skip and Kai and the whole mud-puddle mishap—but he didn't seem all that interested.

"Never mind," he said. "You're gonna get a lot messier anyway."

I followed Gavin down a stone path toward the Dining Hall Annex. I was kind of hoping we'd be riding fancy ATVs, but no such luck. We hoofed it all the way.

The annex was a building with twenty-foot ceilings. Bigger than the dining hall at Hogwarts! It was reserved for fancy stuff like award banquets and Sweet 16 parties and rich-folk family reunions. But this morning it was totally deserted. All the guests were having breakfast next door in the main dining room. I could hear dishes clanking and kids giggling and babies screeching. Gavin pushed through two swinging doors that led from the annex dining room to the annex kitchen. He pointed to my first task:

"Lemur Lad," he said, "meet the flattop!"

The kitchen was almost as big as the dining room. Along one wall was a wide steel cooking griddle. It was gi-normous! Let me just pause here for a size comparison: The flattop in the kitchen at Swifty's Diner was about the size of a card table. This one was about the size of an aircraft carrier. And it looked like it hadn't been cleaned in months! Maybe years. Gavin held up a metal spatula-looking thing with a wooden handle.

"Here's your scraper. Get to it!"

I leaned up against the edge of the flattop and started to push the scraper blade across the metal surface, a few inches at a time. With every push, I brought up a pile of greasy, smelly gunk—enough to make me gag. Suddenly the chimp enclosure didn't seem so bad.

Onion scraps

Burger bits

Cauliflower remnants

Fingernail?

Gavin was right about the mess. Pretty soon the mud on my shirt was the *least* of my worries. I was splattered with charred butter, oily crumbs, and burned food chunks, just for starters. A pair of goggles would have come in handy.

While I was scraping, Gavin was swiping. Every time I glanced over his shoulder I could see him on his Cinder app, flipping left and right, looking for hot Gunkledunk dates. He probably thought he was a real catch. When I looked down the length of the flattop again, it seemed *endless*!

Now, imagine one of those movie scenes where they have the clock on the wall with the hands going around and around to show how much time has gone by. In my head, those hands were going *very* slowly. But before I knew it, it was noon.

It had taken me all morning to get from one end of the flattop to the other. Along the way, I filled two big garbage bags with scrapings. Just when I thought I was finished, Gavin turned on the gas flame under the flattop. He waited until it was sizzling hot. Then he poured a bucket of water on the griddle. The water beaded up and bounced and gave off a huge cloud of steam. It smelled like a food-scrap sauna.

"Now you can get the leftovers!" Gavin said.

Are you kidding me?

I started all over again, this time with hot greasy water splattering on me with every stroke. By the time I had scraped my way down to the end, Gavin had turned off the flames and let the flattop cool down. He ran his finger over the surface.

There was still a little shiny sheen of grease, but he had to admit it was a big improvement.

"Acceptable," he said, "for a greengrub."

"Can I ask you a question?" I said.

"As long as it's short."

"What's a greengrub?"

"It's what they call the junior staff," said Gavin. "Get used to it."

Of course Gavin already had his *own* pet name for me. And he liked that one even more. I was hoping that the flattop scraping might be it for the afternoon. But Gavin wasn't done with me yet. Not by a long shot. Here's a snapshot of the rest of my day one schedule:

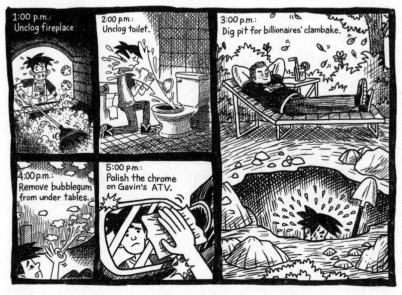

1:00 p.m.: Unclog fireplace

2:00 p.m.: Unclog toilet.

3:00 p.m.: Dig pit for billionaires' clambake.

4:00 p.m.: Remove bubblegum from under tables.

5:00 p.m.: Polish the chrome on Gavin's ATV.

I'm not sure that last one was actually in my job description. But since I never *got* a job description, who knows?

Oh, I forgot. There was lunch in the schedule somewhere. A ham sandwich and some potato chips. Not that I had much of an appetite. My stomach was still a little queasy from the smell of the flattop.

While I polished the chrome on the ATV handlebars to a bright shine, Gavin was still busy on Cinder, lining up a date for the evening. He checked his watch. Finally, he said, "Okay, that's it for the day, Lemur Lad. Wrap it up!" I put the polishing cloth back in the ragbag and wiped my brow. Gavin hopped on his freshly polished ATV and fired it up.

"Get some rest, Lemur Lad!" he shouted over the motor. "You're gonna need it tomorrow!"

I dodged pebbles as he pulled out.

The walk back to my humble abode seemed like a hundred miles. My head ached. My muscles ached. My *bones* ached! And my fingers felt like petrified twigs from all the scraping and plunging and digging and polishing. I was caked in mud and grease and soot and sand and who knows what else. I smelled like an onion wrapped in garlic, then rolled in ashes and dunked in a toilet.

Could this job get any *more* gross?

Based on my luck so far, what do *you* think?

CHAPTER 32

BOTTOMS UP!

More scraping? Really??? The very next morning, I was lying on my back under a sailboat named the *Buckaroo,* which belonged to Mr. Malarkey, one of the richest guests at Green Banks. Technically, the *Buckaroo* was a sloop—which, according to Gavin, was different from a ketch, which was different from a cutter. A sloop has one mast. A ketch has two. A cutter has three. Who knew? Until that morning, my main experience with sailing was watching the *Pirates of the Caribbean* movies, so this was all fresh info to me. And to be honest, it didn't matter much from where I was lying. The bottom of one boat pretty much looks like any other.

The sloop hung from big chains over a long wooden dock at the marina, leaving just a couple of feet of space underneath. My job was scraping lake scum from the hull—the part that's usually underwater. And it was not pretty down there!

I was using a tool that looked like a screwdriver with a wide blade at the end. A pump sprayer and some suspicious-smelling chemicals were also involved. As I worked, chunks of greenish-brown gunk fell onto my shirt, my shorts, and my face. I'm no marine biologist, but I think it was algae. All I know for sure is that it was *disgusting*. And possibly poisonous. I was worried about catching Lake Scum Syndrome. I didn't know if that was a real thing, but it definitely *could* be. Maybe I'd be the first one to come down with it, and then doctors would have to name it after me. "Khatchadorian Lake Scum Syndrome!" My claim to fame! My picture in medical books! A plaque in the science room at Hills Village Middle School! Trust me, a lot of weird thoughts go through your brain when you're on your back under a dirty boat.

By nine a.m. the marina was humming with

activity. I heard boat motors starting and people saying "Cast off!" (Whatever *that* means.) When I turned my head to the side, I could see the legs of the rich and famous passing by on their way to a pleasant day of water-skiing or parasailing.

I heard a rumor once that Michelangelo painted the whole ceiling of the Sistine Chapel while he was lying on his back. I don't know if it's true, but I think it might have been easier than this. And at least he got a masterpiece out of it. Not me. Whenever I thought I'd gotten to the end of the gunk, a whole new layer seemed to show up. And each layer was more gross than the last one. The *Buckaroo* was thirty feet long, and so far I'd only covered about two lousy feet. I was hot and sweaty and miserable.

I guess that's when I got sloppy.

I was working on one really stubborn patch when my scraper slipped. A big wad of green gunk flew out from under the boat and hit one of the guests—right on the leg of his clean white Bermuda shorts! When he bent over to inspect the damage, his big butt knocked a tall stack of life preservers off the dock and into the lake. Good thing they floated. I couldn't hear exactly what Sloppy Shorts said at first, but I'm pretty sure you couldn't print it in a book like this anyway. The next thing I heard was Gavin apologizing profusely. Then I heard the guest loud and clear—a deep voice with a Southern drawl.

"Ah say, Gavin! Mah shorts are done foah! Ah'm sendin' Mistah Pincus the bill! Y'all better tell your greengrub to be moah careful!"

The voice walked off. Gavin bent his face down under the boat and hissed at me.

"Nice going, Lemur Lad! You just slimed a senator!"

Great. With my luck, the FBI would be knocking on my cabin door tonight, hauling me to jail for senator-sliming. Could this summer get any worse?

CHAPTER 33

SLIP-SLIDING AWAY

emur Lad! Bus table ten!"

Gavin was barking orders at me from his station near the kitchen. While he barked, he also plucked *pommes frites* off guest plates as the waiters carried them out to the Green Banks dining room. At dinnertime, Gavin was what they called the service captain. That means he was the boss of all the greengrubs with lowly dining room jobs. And the jobs didn't get any lower than mine. I was a busboy. Not sure what it had to do with a bus, but it meant I had to pick up all the dirty dishes and table scraps after the rich guests were done eating, then carry the whole mess back to the kitchen. I wasn't allowed to talk to the guests or even look them in the eye. Not that they would have noticed me anyway. They were too busy bragging about golf scores, European vacations, and which private schools their kids just got into—not to mention filling their pie holes with really fancy food.

Menu

Baby Artichokes
Stuffed with baby cauliflower
Stuffed with baby mushrooms

Pheasant Paté
with caviar gravy

Artisanal Kumquats
in llama milk

I wore a short white jacket and carried a big black plastic tub, which got really heavy with all the plates and glasses and leftover food. Pretty disgusting too. The poop-flinging chimps were neater than this crowd. And the waste! The food these folks left on their plates could feed a starving continent. Maybe two.

The guests at table ten were already heading out the door when I got to their table. I started dumping everything into my tub—half-gnawed pork chops, leftover asparagus tips, partly nibbled bread sticks, and wet cigars. (There was no smoking in the dining room, but that didn't stop rich guys from sticking cigars in their mouths after a meal just to look important.)

I was picking up a dish of barely touched truffle-infused mashed potatoes when I heard laughing from a few tables over. The laughing sounded familiar…Where had I heard it before? I glanced over and saw Skip and Kai, the hoverboard kings. They were digging into Green Banks Signature Sundaes, topped with vanilla-flavored whipped cream and "delicate shavings of rich Belgian chocolate." Whatever happened to sprinkles?

I hoisted my heavy bus bucket with both arms and headed back toward the kitchen. I tried to walk smoothly so the dishes wouldn't clatter too much. Busboys were supposed to be barely seen and never heard. I wore thick rubber-soled shoes and tried to move like a ghost. Gavin gave demerits for excessive clinking.

But somehow, when I was almost past Skip and Kai's table, a big spoonful of whipped cream ended up on the floor in front of me. Accident? You be the judge. All I know is, as soon as my foot hit the slippery goop, I went sailing across the dining hall like I was wearing roller skates. My bucket flew into the air. Dirty plates and cold leftovers crashed and plopped onto the tables of guests who were still eating.

I tried to catch my balance, but it was no use.
The next thing I knew, I was doing a face plant into
Mrs. Malarkey's gooseberry pie. *Splat!*

"Hey!" said Mr. Malarkey. "Aren't you the kid
who slimed the senator?"

Once again, I was famous—for all the wrong
reasons.

CHAPTER 34

PICTURE PERFECT

Early the next morning, after my busing privileges
had been temporarily revoked, I stepped out
onto the porch to breathe in the morning air. Georgia
was inside enjoying her daily dose of Krispie Krackles
cereal, and Mom had her painting easel set up out
front, like she did every morning. She liked to catch
the rays just as they started coming through the
leaves. "Golden light," she called it.

I sat on one of the beat-up wooden porch chairs, which felt like it might collapse at any minute. I sipped my OJ and hoped I wouldn't get a splinter in my butt.

Mom looked so happy with a brush in her hand. I knew how much she loved painting. She even named me after a famous artist: Raffaello Sanzio da Urbino. No joke. You can Google him. I love art too, but at the moment, I felt like I was only good at the art of making things worse. I had a serious question on my mind, and there was only one person I trusted to answer it.

"Mom," I said, "when is it okay to quit something?"

I knew she heard me, but she kept right on painting. She was adding some extra blue to the sky at the top of her picture. Sometimes it took Mom a minute or so to come up with an answer. But it was always worth the wait.

"Well, Rafe," she said, still studying her sky, "we all feel like quitting sometimes. I know *I* do. But like I told your sister once—you're a Khatchadorian. We don't always have it easy in life, but we don't give up either."

She looked over at me. "Is there something we need to talk about?"

I shook my head and polished off my OJ. No sense in rehashing last night's disaster, even though it took two showers to get all the gooseberry gunk out of my hair.

"Just asking," I said. Maybe I already knew what the answer was going to be, but I just needed to hear it out loud. The last thing I wanted to do was surrender and cast a permanent shadow over the Khatchadorian name. That doesn't mean I felt confident. Far from it. Because I knew there were *other* ways of leaving a job besides quitting.

As I headed down the path, I thought about the various ways I might meet my end, and how they might ship my body home. Maybe they'd just tie me to the roof of the car. I was pretty sure Gavin had it in for me because I was making him look bad.

And I was about to make him look even *worse*.

CHAPTER 35

GLUB, GLUB!

I made up my mind that this was the morning I was going to redeem myself and show Gavin and all the super-rich guests what I was really made of. Khatchadorian Strong!

Gavin had said to meet him at the marina first thing. I looked forward to the fresh lake breeze. Maybe I'd even get to take a little dip.

Be careful what you wish for.

It was the morning of the annual Green Banks Regatta—when all the guests with sailboats raced from the marina to Baker's Point and back again while all the guests with powerboats just watched and clapped (there weren't any guests who *didn't* own some kind of boat). The winning team got their name engraved on a huge trophy that sat in a glass case in the dining room. It was a pretty big deal, if you're into that kind of thing.

For the past week, all the sailing teams had been practicing like crazy, yelling stuff like "Stand by to come about!" and "Lee ho!" I figured out that ropes are called *lines* (but sometimes *sheets*, which made *no* sense). Toward the front of a boat was *forward*. But toward the back was aft. Why not *backward*? I guess when you're rich, you have time to memorize all this stuff, but it was pretty confusing to an innocent bystander like me.

When I arrived at the marina, Gavin was leaning against a wooden post, chatting with a girl in a white blouse, white pants, and a sailing cap. I wondered if he found her on Cinder. Probably not. She looked rich. And rich people probably have their own private dating app to keep out the riffraff. As soon as Gavin noticed me, he started to act all commander-like to impress the sailing girl.

"Lemur Lad!" he shouted. "I need you to back

Mr. Malarkey's boat down the ramp!" He meant the cement ramp that led right down into the lake. The idea was to back the boat trailer into the water just deep enough so that the boat would float.

Earlier that morning, Mr. Malarkey had been practicing with his crew on Lake Adolfson a few miles away, probably coming up with some spiffy new nautical moves. Now he was at the end of the dock talking shop with some of his fellow captains. From the look of him, you'd never guess Mr. Malarkey was a supermogul. He was short and kind of goofy-looking, with a big gap between his two front teeth. But his company, Malarkey Media, was so huge even *kids* had heard of it. Me included. *Never judge a book by its cover*, Grandma Dotty always says.

The *Buckaroo* sat on top of a trailer attached to a huge white SUV, with the rear end of the boat (sorry, the *stern*) angled toward the lake. I was about to tell Gavin I was too young to drive, but why bother? He'd just ignore me. And maybe the driving laws were a little looser up here in the woods.

I saw Skip and Kai watching from the dock as I opened the car door. It was really heavy! Probably bulletproof. The engine was already running, even though it was so quiet you could hardly tell. I slid into the driver's seat and checked out the instrument panel. It looked like a fighter jet. I ran my fingers over the shift knob—all shiny and cool-looking. I put my hands on the steering wheel. The leather was as soft as a baby's bottom—if your baby was made of leather.

I had to slouch down in the seat and stretch out my legs to reach the pedals, which made my head lower than the steering wheel. But this was no time to panic. I'd watched Mom drive a car thousands of times. How hard could it be? Right pedal GO. Left pedal STOP. Pretty easy, right? Sure it is. When you're going straight ahead. It turns out that when you're backing up, everything looks different. Somebody really should have warned me about that.

"Just put it in reverse, slowpoke!" Gavin had his hands on his hips. I guess he thought it made him look cooler. But it only made him look meaner.

I pulled the gear knob down until I saw a big fat *R* light up on the dashboard. I looked into the side mirror. I could see the edge of the trailer and the hull of the *Buckaroo* behind me. And then I felt the whole setup—trailer, boat, and car—rolling backward. Too fast! I put my foot on the brake. At least I *thought* it was the brake.

It wasn't. It was the go-superfast pedal.

Like I said, I was looking behind me. Also, I don't have a great sense of direction. The car leaped backward, lurching me into the steering wheel painfully. You would think my foot would've lurched off the gas pedal too, but it was frozen in place.

At moments like that, a lot of images pop into your mind, like a series of tiny Instagram photos. Here's what I saw:

I felt the dock whizzing by like a movie running backward. I heard a rumble, then a splash, then a loud gurgle. There might have been a few screams mixed in there too. I stomped on the brake pedal. Got the right one this time. The boat was in the lake, for sure. Good job. But so was the car! Right up to the bottom of its fancy power windows.

I remember thinking that a guy as rich as Mr. Malarkey probably had a few cars in his fleet. Maybe he wouldn't miss this one. I also remember wondering if it was actually possible to mess up two jobs in one summer.

If anyone could do it, it was yours truly.

CHAPTER 36

VIEW FROM THE TOP

Rafe! You're home early!"

Mom was still painting when she saw me coming up the trail. Georgia was swinging in a hammock between two trees, reading *The Phantom Tollbooth*. Right away, she noticed that I was soaked from the waist down. Not much gets past my sister.

"Have you been wading for clams?" she said.

"Not exactly," I said. "I don't want to talk about it."

I went into the cabin and wrung the lake water out of my socks while I reflected on the whole sad morning. Naturally, after the "incident," they called Mr. Pincus down to the dock. But he wasn't as mad at me as I expected. He calmed Mr. Malarkey down and "suggested" that I take a day or two off to let the dust settle. "Spend some time with the family" was the way he put it. As a matter of fact, Gavin got into *more* trouble for letting me drive the car in the first place. I heard something about "docking his pay." Sounded like the right term, under the circumstances.

When Mom came into the bedroom to check on me, I was standing in my wet underpants. Not a good look. I slammed the door.

"Are you going back to work?" Mom said from the other side.

"Nope," I said. "I have a couple of days off." I didn't want to tell her why. I figured she'd find out soon enough.

"Perfect!" she said. "It's a great afternoon for a family outing!"

"Yes!!!" I heard Georgia say. "I'm soooooo bored!" I kind of understood. A few weeks in the woods sounds great on paper, but my sister is the type who needs constant stimulation. She missed her friends, and the Wi-Fi in the cabin was practically nonexistent. She couldn't even follow her favorite math bloggers. Collecting fireflies in jars was fun for a night or two. But let's face it, when you've seen one firefly, you've seen them all.

I put on a dry pair of shorts and a fresh T-shirt—one that did *not* say STAFF on both sides. I felt like myself again. When I opened the door, Mom was already packing a picnic lunch: peanut butter and jelly sandwiches, potato chips, a bag of vanilla wafers, and a few bootlegged bottles of Zoom soda from Swifty's. Georgia tossed in a box of Krispie Krackles. I guess they're not just for breakfast anymore.

After all that time just sitting under the trees, I wasn't sure the trusty Khatchadorianmobile would even start up. But it did. On the first try. Mom backed out of the parking spot (she made it look so easy) and headed down the trail.

I realized how much Mom and Georgia needed a change of scenery. I'd been busy all the time and even learned a few new skills, such as how deep to dig a clambake pit (about three feet) and what kind of polish to use on ATV handlebars (Healey's KromeGlo). Mom enjoyed painting, but she was probably getting tired of the view from our cabin. A little getaway would be nice for everybody.

Getting out of Green Banks was a lot easier than getting in. When we pulled up to the big front gate, it opened automatically. We drove right through. Pretty soon we were on a winding road, heading for the other side of the lake. Georgia had started to put in her earbuds when Mom looked in the rearview mirror and said, "Hey! Let's be together today, okay?"

"We *are* together," said Georgia. "I can smell Rafe's feet."

"I mean fully present," said Mom, "enjoying each other's company. Not off in our own little worlds." She switched on the car radio. It started blasting "Can't Stop the Feeling!" Justin Timberlake's voice sounded all funky and friendly. Say what you want about JT—the man knows how to set a mood. Mom turned it up to concert volume and started singing along.

"I got this feelin' inside my bones—it goes electric wavy when I turn it on!"

Usually Georgia and I get really embarrassed when Mom starts singing and doing her shoulder shimmy, but for some reason it felt pretty sweet right now. Maybe it was the altitude. Georgia started singing along too. Then Mom and Georgia began doing harmony. Of course, I didn't know any of the words (I'm more of a hip-hop fan), so I just started tapping out the beat on my leg. If anybody had seen us rocking out in our car like that, they would have said we were crazy. But we didn't pass a single human being. And who cares what the squirrels thought.

I need my noise-canceling nuts!

When we got to the other side of the lake, Mom pulled up onto a little hill that overlooked the water. "Perfect spot!" she said. And it was. Mom was an ace at picnic-spot picking. It's almost like she went to school for it. We opened up the cooler, unwrapped our goodies, and started feasting. A sandwich and a cold sip of Zoom soda never tasted so good.

Way below us in the water, we saw some kayakers and windsurfers, and a bunch of sailboats cruising across the lake in a long line. Pretty as a picture.

Hold on. Not cruising. *Racing!* It was the Green Banks Regatta! I ran back to the car to get Grandma Dotty's bird-watching binoculars.

From the top of the hill, I had the perfect view. There was a good wind and the sails on the boats were all billowed out. The crews scampered around the decks like busy little ants. I could see the big orange buoy that marked the turn at Baker's Point. Two boats fought for the lead. They were neck and neck heading for the turn. Then, all of a sudden, one boat swung its sail around to catch an extra blast of wind. It made a tight curve around the buoy and headed back toward the marina while the other crew scrambled to catch up. The leading boat had blue-and-white sails—and I'd know that hull anywhere. Go, *Buckaroo!* I guess I hadn't done any damage. At least to the boat.

CHAPTER 37

THINGS THAT GO "GRRRR!" IN THE NIGHT

After the picnic, Mom drove back to Green Banks the long way. *Really* long. We crossed covered bridges. We passed abandoned hunting lodges. We filled up at a gas station that had one pump and an old guy who actually wiped our windshield. I think the GPS might have gone wacky at some point, because we definitely made a few wrong turns. But that's life in the wilderness. And we were in no hurry anyway.

You're on your own.

By the time we got back to our cabin, it was dark and my sister was fast asleep in the backseat. Mom parked the car, then scooped Georgia up and carried her into the cabin like a sack of birdseed. When we got into the bedroom, Georgia perked up just enough to climb into her bunk. My face was sunburned from hanging out the window all day, and I think I might have swallowed a few mosquitos. But I felt better than I had in a long time. Mom kissed me on the forehead and said good night. When she shut the door, the room was totally black.

As I closed my eyes, I heard something in the trees outside the window. It was an owl hooting. Which reminded me of Lila. Which reminded me of Penelope. But those pleasant memories were drowned out by another sound—my sister snoring. I lifted my foot and kicked the bottom of Georgia's mattress. Cue another dead moth shower. And that's the last thing I remember, until...

...hours later...

...in the dead of night...

"Pssst! Did you hear that?"

Was I dreaming? Nope. It was Georgia for real. I opened one eye and saw her head dangling upside down from her bunk. A very disturbing image when you're half asleep.

"Hear *what*?" I mumbled.

"Listen!"

I leaned up on my elbows and rubbed my eyes. I listened. At first—nothing. Then I heard it too. It was a low, rumbling sound with a little echo at the end.

"It's coming from across the lake!" said Georgia.

"Probably just a bear in the woods," I said. "Go back to sleep!"

"Bears don't growl," said Georgia. "They grunt—or they huff. I saw it on Animal Planet." Great. Now *she's* the wildlife expert.

"We gotta investigate," she said. She slid down her ladder butt-first and landed on the floor with a little thump.

"What *I* gotta do...is *sleep*!" I said. I flopped my head back on the pillow.

Georgia pulled on her pants and a sweatshirt, put on her shoes, and tiptoed out of the bedroom toward the front door.

Then I heard it again. The faraway growl.

Georgia poked her head back in. "You a scaredy-cat?"

"No way!"

Actually, I was. Sometimes. Kind of. But I wasn't about to let my kid sister know it. And besides, I had the only flashlight. I kept it under my pillow for emergencies. And this was turning into one. Because Georgia was already outside, heading for a dark trail that led into the woods.

I hopped out of bed and put on my shoes. I tiptoed out of the cabin so Mom wouldn't hear.

"I'm coming," I whispered loudly. "But only to keep you from falling into the water."

Famous almost-last words.

CHAPTER 38

JUST A WALK IN THE DARK

Watch out! That's poison ivy over there!" said Georgia.

"How can you even *see* that?" I asked. I had the flashlight beam pointed straight ahead. Georgia was looking in the bushes to the side. Turns out my sister has excellent night vision.

"Leaves of three, let it be," she said. Good tip.

We'd been hiking for a half hour on a narrow path that snaked around the edge of the lake. "Probably an ancient Native American trail," said Georgia. Maybe so, but ancient Native Americans probably had more sense than to roam around in the dark. At this hour, they'd all be snuggled in their wigwams.

By now, we were so far from Green Banks that

we couldn't even see the green light at the edge of the dock. From here, the lake looked really misty and spooky, like in a horror movie just before the arm of the dead camper reaches up to flip the canoe.

Who knows what lurks beneath?

Just then, something grabbed my arm! I jumped about five feet! But it was only Georgia. She held her finger over her lips.

There it was again. The growl. But this time it sounded a lot louder. And a lot closer. We crept up a few more yards, pushing branches aside as we went. When we came to a thick row of bushes, we stopped. We listened. Whatever was making the noise was coming from the other side! What could it be?

The Usual Suspects

This might be a good time to emphasize that it's really dumb to go wandering in the woods at night without adult supervision. And it's even dumber to try tracking down the sound of a mysterious wild beast. But if you've been following my life so far, you know that I'm not known for great judgment. So when Georgia jumped through the bushes, I jumped right after her...

"Owww!"

...and ended up with my face squished against a chain link fence.

Georgia was squished right up next to me—so close I could hear her heart beating. Or maybe it was *my* heart, beating twice as loud. It does that sometimes.

I lost my flashlight and had to go back and grab it out of a pricker patch. I guess the batteries were running low, because the beam had gone from bright white to dim yellow. But there was still enough to make out the scene. As my namesake Raffaello would say, let me paint the picture for you:

The fence right in front of us was rusty and twisted, and some of the metal posts holding it up tilted sideways. It looked like a strong breeze might blow the whole thing over. On the other side of the fence, there was some bare dirt and scrubby grass, like somebody tried to grow a lawn and gave up. I moved the beam of the flashlight along the ground. We saw a couple of beat-up buckets, some rope, and a few wooden barrels. Then the beam hit a big box. We heard the growl again—like a giant clearing his throat.

I tapped Georgia on the shoulder and pointed left. We shifted a few feet down the fence for a better angle. I shined the flashlight in the direction of the box again. Except now we could see that it wasn't a box.

It was a cage!

All of a sudden, from inside, we saw two glowing eyes looking back at us! Then we saw a brownish-gold shape with a huge head.

"Holy safari!" said Georgia. "It's a lion! A real one!" As usual, she was right.

The big cat almost filled the whole cage. Its long tail twitched against the wooden wall and sometimes it flicked out through the bars. There was barely enough room for the poor guy to turn around. Forget king of the jungle. This guy was in solitary confinement. If I were in his situation, I'd growl too.

"Shine it up there!" said Georgia. She pointed to the top of the cage on the side closest to us. I moved the flashlight beam. I scrunched my eyes. There was some lettering on the wood, all scratched up and faded. It said:

PROPERTY OF CONGO PARK

Georgia lifted her head, but I pulled her back down again. Because I heard *another* noise coming from the shadows on the other side of the fence. Georgia squeezed up next to me. Then she heard it too!

"Maybe this was a mistake," she whispered. You *think*?

CHAPTER 39

HEADED FOR BOOT HILL

Crunch, crunch, crunch, crunch!
Footsteps! Georgia and I crouched down.
Where's that invisibility cloak when you need it?
We were both curled up into little balls, our noses
pressed into the dirt. The footsteps were coming
closer! I lifted my head a little. Then, out of the
darkness, I saw a pair of big black leather boots
coming toward the fence, right where we were
hiding. Tall ones. All smeared with mud.
Crunch, crunch, crunch, crunch!
I held my breath. So did Georgia. The boots
stopped right in front of us. Game over. I wondered
how it would feel to be fed to a hungry lion. After
all my crazy middle school mishaps, this was my
big finish. I just hoped it would be over in a hurry.

A couple of bites at most, with minimal chewing.

Then...the boots started walking away! Whoever it was did NOT have excellent night vision. Because we were basically right there in front of him.

I'm surprised he didn't smell us. Or me, anyway. Because when I get scared, I get a little gassy. Sorry. I know. Too much information.

We heard the boot sounds fading away into the shadows past the lion cage.

Crunch, crunch! Crunch, crunch! Crunch, crunch!

We lifted our heads and looked at each other. Georgia had a big spot of dirt on her nose. I probably did too.

We didn't say anything. Not a word. We crawled back through the bushes and ran back down the trail, with me leading the way. I didn't even bother to turn on the flashlight. It was like all my animal instincts had returned. I hopped over roots and branches like nobody's business. We got back to the cabin in half the time! We were both wheezing like marathoners at the finish line. After we'd caught our breath a little, we tiptoed inside and back into our bedroom. Georgia climbed up the ladder and flopped onto her back. Another dead moth shower.

"You know what we have to do tomorrow, right?" she whispered.

"Absolutely," I whispered back.

For once, my annoying sister and I were on the same page.

CHAPTER 40

AIN'T TOO PROUD TO BEG

What did you two scamps get into last night?"
The next morning at the kitchen table,
Mom plucked a leafy twig out of Georgia's hair. I
tried to hide my dirty face behind a paper towel.

"And Rafe, what's with those scratches on your
arm?"

I thought fast. "Probably from scrubbing the
inside of Mr. Malarkey's head," I said. Mom looked
at me like I'd lost my noodles.

"That's a boat toilet," said Georgia. I wasn't the
only one who'd picked up some nautical terms.

"Well, go wash up before you eat, both of you!
You look like you've been dragged through the
woods!"

Georgia and I couldn't even look at each other as we headed for the bathroom.

When we were all cleaned up, we sat back down at the table. Since I had the day off, Mom put out a real spread—a farm breakfast, she called it. We had scrambled eggs and bacon, toast with jelly, and a crumb cake with cinnamon sugar topping. Mom sipped a cup of coffee and flipped through a catalog from an art museum. That's when Georgia went to work on her. She leaned forward and put on her best sweet face.

Head tilted

Eyes wide

Maximum dimples

She patted Mom's hand. She even made her voice sound cute and irresistible. I have to admit, my sister can really turn on the charm when it suits her purpose—which, at the moment, was also *my* purpose. Because we both wanted exactly the same thing.

"Mom, can you please, please, please, *please,* take us to Congo Park today?" said Georgia. I thought it was one *please* too many, but never question a pro.

Mom put down her coffee. She closed her catalog. "Congo Park?" she said. "What's that?"

Georgia sank the hook. "We don't know yet," she said, "but we *have* to find out!"

"It might be the most exciting place we've ever seen!" I said. Probably an exaggeration—but I wasn't taking any chances. I needed to close the deal.

"In that case," said Mom, "how can I say no?"

CHAPTER 41

JUNGLE BUNGLE

As we pulled up, we noticed that the Congo Park sign was dangling off-center from a pair of fake vines—and a couple of important letters were missing.

"Are you guys *sure* this is where you want to go?" asked Mom. Georgia and I both nodded. "Yep!" "Definitely!" We needed answers—and this was the place to find them.

At least the price was right. Five bucks apiece for kids under five feet—and we both definitely qualified. Mom had done some research and found a landmark creek nearby that she was dying to paint, which meant we'd be on our own for the whole morning. She reached into her purse and handed me a ten-dollar bill for admission and gave us each another ten bucks for spending money. Then she tapped me on the forehead, like she always does when she wants me to pay special attention.

"Look after your sister," she said. "And don't talk to strangers. I'll pick you up right here at one o'clock! Got it?"

"Loud and clear!" I said.

"Happy painting!" said Georgia. We waved to Mom as she pulled away. Then we paid our admission and walked through a green plastic tunnel into darkest Africa—at least that's what the sign said.

When we came out the other side, we could tell that Congo Park had seen better days. And that's putting it mildly. From the other end of the park, we could hear loud rattling and scraping metal. It was the giant CongoCoaster—and it sounded like it was about to go off the rails any second.

"No way I'm getting on *that* thing," said Georgia—and she was usually pretty adventurous. Normally, I might have been tempted by Jungle Snake Cove or King Butu's Diamond Pit, but today I had a one-track mind. And Georgia was on the same track. We had a *lion* to find! We knew he was here somewhere. But *where*?

"Don't miss the Jungle Show. Filled with thrills and excitement," said a whiny little voice. We both turned around. Jungle Show? Jackpot!

The whiny voice belonged to a tall, skinny teenage girl in a safari outfit. She had her red hair pulled back in a ponytail under a Yankees sun visor, and she carried a little canvas bag slung over her shoulder. It was early in the day and she already had a touch of sunburn on her cheeks and nose. Her name tag said HI! I'M CONGO KIM! She reached into her canvas bag and handed us a couple of brochures.

Typical Congo Park Employee

Stooped posture →

Vacant eyes

Sore feet

"Prepare for a world of daring and danger," she said. Note the lack of exclamation points. She wasn't selling hard at all. We could tell her heart just wasn't in it.

"Which way?" asked Georgia. Congo Kim stretched out a skinny arm and pointed to a muddy path just past the Savannah Souvenir & Bait Shop.

We followed the path down to a separate area behind the main park—away from the clatter of the CongoCoaster. I noticed Congo Kim strolling along the fence at the end of the seating section. She was busy on her cell phone. I figured she'd probably seen this show about a thousand times. But this was our first rodeo—so to speak—and we couldn't wait!

CHAPTER 42

THE MANE ATTRACTION

Ladies and gentlemen and children of all ages!" said the ringmaster in a booming voice. Actually, it was just a recording from a rusty speaker hanging from a light pole. But I got a tingle all the same.

"Please direct your *sfzzzzzbt!* to the center ring!" instructed the recording, through flashes of loud static. There was only one ring. It was about thirty feet across, with heavy black bars all the way around. Inside the ring on one side was a straw hut with a thin curtain for a door. The sound from the speaker went in and out. There was a lot of static.

"Introducing a man who doesn't know the meaning of *sfzzzzzbt*! Recently returned from a

tour of the grand capitals of *sfzzzzzbt*...lion tamer extraordinaire—Monsieur François DeFarge! *Sfzzzzzbt!*"

Georgia and I craned our necks. We were literally on the edge of our seats.

The curtain parted and then...there he was! The master of beasts! He strutted to the center of the ring with his nose in the air—and black leather boots on his feet!

Where have we seen these before?

"Look!" I whispered to Georgia. "It's the *guy*!"

Monsieur DeFarge strutted around the ring a couple of times, cracking a long black whip. It made a sound like a firecracker each time it snapped. Finally, he stood still and pointed his whip at a small covered tunnel at the other side of the ring. We'd hardly noticed it at first. He yelled something in French. Suddenly, out of the tunnel walked a real-life lion, shaking his head and roaring!

Georgia elbowed me so hard I almost fell off the bench. "That's *him!*" she said. "That's our *lion!*" The roar definitely sounded familiar. After the lion came out of the tunnel, he stopped and sat back on his haunches. DeFarge kept cracking his whip. The lion looked like he would rather be anywhere else.

Then DeFarge started shouting stuff in French—it kind of sounded like swear words to me. The lion shuffled over to a platform and hopped on top of it. The lion tamer turned to the crowd and held his hands up in victory, like this was some kind of great trick.

The audience was getting restless. You could see cocker spaniels doing cooler stuff than this on YouTube any day of the week.

"This is pathetic!" said Georgia. She started to stand up. I pulled her back down. I knew just how she felt. I'd never felt sorrier for an animal in my life. But we couldn't just leave. After coming this far, we had to see what happened next.

After two or three minutes of making the lion do more platform-hopping, DeFarge picked up a huge hoop from the side of the ring. Then he pulled a lighter out of his pocket and flicked the flame on. He held the flame aloft like the Statue of Liberty. The audience perked up. This looked promising.

He touched the flame to the ring and suddenly a stream of fire raced around the outside. Pretty awesome!

Actual ring

Actual fire

Actual lion

Do NOT try this at home!

He held the ring of fire up in front of the lion. The lion blinked a few times. Maybe he was nearsighted. Or maybe just a little nervous. Can you blame him? The lion tamer cracked the whip in the air. Once! Twice! Three times! On the third crack the lion crouched down on his platform— then launched himself right through the flaming ring! He must have covered about fifteen feet in the air!

Okay. I admit this part was pretty exciting— and pretty scary. And it was obviously the big finale, because circus music started blaring from the speaker, and the lion tamer did a corny showbiz bow.

The lion circled the ring once and headed back toward the little tunnel he'd come out of. He stuck his head in, then pulled it back out—like he was having second thoughts. He didn't seem to be in any hurry to go from a big cage back to a little one. The next time he stuck his head in, the lion tamer gave him a swift kick in the rump. The lion gave up and went into the tunnel. Not everybody saw that last part.

Most families were already packing up their strollers and sippy cups. But *I* saw it.

So did Georgia. And I'd never seen her so mad!

CHAPTER 43

THE ART OF THE COMPLIMENT

S o, did you guys have a great time?" asked
Mom as we slid into the backseat. I could tell
she was in a really cheery mood. It seemed like a
morning by herself had done her a world of good!
Georgia plopped down with her arms folded. She
was still ticked off about the lion. But I decided
to put on a smiley face. (Plus, our mission wasn't
complete—not by a long shot!)

"It was great!" I said. "We can't wait to come
back!"

Georgia shot me a death stare. I shook my head
just enough to communicate that she should keep
her yap shut. And for once, she did.

"Well, I had a pretty great morning myself,"

Mom said. "Take a look in the back and tell me what you think!"

I flipped around and leaned over the top of the backseat. Right there in the cargo area, Mom had her new painting lying faceup on top of an old sheet. Some of the paint was still wet and shiny. The picture was of a little silver creek winding through a grove of tall trees. The light came through the leaves just so.

Golden light!

"Wow! That's really good, Mom!" I said.

Georgia popped her head up right next to mine.

"Sweet! You should change your name to Julia van Gogh!" she said.

"Look down in the lower right corner," Mom said, peeking at us in the rearview mirror. Georgia and I leaned in closer to the painting. Tucked under a bush in the corner of the scene, Mom had painted two cute little chipmunks with chubby cheeks.

"Awwwww!" said Georgia. "Adorbs!"

"I call them Rafe and Georgia!" said Mom.

"So cool!" said Georgia. "Can I hang it in my bedroom at home? Please?"

"We'll see," said Mom.

I sat back down and fastened my seat belt. "I think we should sell it for a hundred thousand dollars!" I said.

Mom laughed as she started the car. "Gosh! You kids are being so *nice*!" she said. "I should bring you to Congo Park more often!"

BACK TO THE GRIND

I thought maybe after a short vacation away from me, Gavin might be a little nicer. But on my first morning back at work, he was as mean as ever. Maybe even meaner.

"Grab those bags, Lemur Lad!"

My first job of the day was hauling big sacks of coffee beans from the loading dock to the roasting room near the kitchen. In case you're wondering, I was still banned from the marina. So I was doing a lot of inside work for the time being.

It's a statistical fact that rich people like really expensive coffee. And to keep his guests happy, Mr. Pincus always bought the world's rarest beans—which came in the world's heaviest bags. Each one was like dragging a dead body. (Not that

I ever had to drag a dead body. Just want to make that clear.)

Rafe: 90 lbs.   Sack: 100 lbs.

It wouldn't have hurt Gavin to toss a sack or two over his shoulder. Unlike me, he was *built* for hauling dead bodies. But once again, he was just tapping his phone, still busy on Cinder. I hoped just one girl would right-swipe him so he would put his phone away and help me out. But I knew it was a long shot.

After I got all the sacks into the roasting room, I had to open them up, pour the beans into a metal pail, and then climb a ladder to load the beans into the funnel at the top of the giant Kafino King industrial roaster. This thing looked like a time machine out of a comic book—about ten feet tall, with chrome trim and all kinds of fancy dials and knobs, and a big rounded belly where the roasting actually happened.

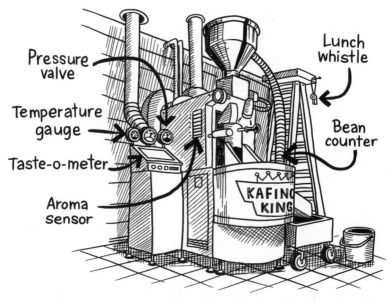

Pressure valve

Temperature gauge

Taste-o-meter

Aroma sensor

Lunch whistle

Bean counter

KAFINO KING

If you like the smell of coffee, I guess this would be your idea of heaven. For me, it didn't come close to the heavenly aroma of a fresh-baked Swifty's pie.

As soon as that thought came into my head, I started to feel a little homesick. I wondered what

Flip and all my other friends were doing back in Hills Village right now. As if there were any question. They were playing Wormhole, of course! Polishing their moves. Tweaking their strategies. Perfecting their hand-eye coordination. By the time I got back, my skill level would be back to Newbie Negative, or lower! Like the saying goes, use it or lose it.

Then I started thinking about what Penelope was up to. I wondered if Lila had graduated from chicken strips to steak. I wondered if Abel the giraffe had had her baby yet. My mind started wandering. I was thinking about all the great stuff I was missing. And, as Grandma Dotty would say, that's when things started to go south.

After I dumped in my third pail of beans, the machine gave a shudder and started to make little gagging noises.

"Nice one, Lemur Lad," said Gavin. "You just jammed the funnel aperture!"

"What do I do now?" I asked.

"Whack it!" said Gavin.

Personally, I thought we should consult the manual, but Gavin sounded like he knew what he was talking about. I gave the funnel a couple of hard slaps with my hand. No good. If anything, the gagging got *worse*! A bunch of beans were stuck in the funnel and they were clogging up the whole contraption.

"Harder!" said Gavin. "You need to get the thing moving!" You'd think a machine this classy would come with a big golden hammer for problems like this. But I didn't see one. I looked down at Gavin.

"Toss me your shoe," I said.

"My what?"

"I need something heavy!" I said. "Toss me your shoe!" My shoe size was 6.

Gavin was a 10 at least. He knew it was the right idea. He unlaced his left SuperTread trainer and threw it up to me.

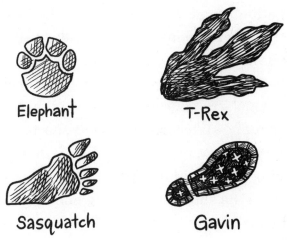

Elephant

T-Rex

Sasquatch

Gavin

I held the shoe by the toe and starting whacking the top of the funnel. On about the fourth whack, the machine stopped gagging and started humming again. That's when I saw Gavin's shoe liner come loose and drop inside the funnel.

Oops.

I tried to grab it, but it was too late! I watched it get sucked down the tube into the roaster. I looked for a panic button. Didn't see one. Started to panic. I peeked down into the funnel. The beans were flowing. The shoe liner was already gone. Nothing I could do. Chalk it up to experience. Lucky for me, Gavin was too busy on his phone to see my slipup.

I came down the ladder and handed Gavin back his shoe, minus the liner. He slipped it back on, balancing on one foot while keeping his eyes on his phone screen. Would he notice that he was now about one-sixteenth of an inch shorter on his left side? Not now, he wouldn't. Not with what was happening on his Cinder app!

"Yessss!" he shouted in his big honking voice. "About time!"

I guess miracles *do* happen.

Gavin Groose had just scored a *date*!

CHAPTER 45

BELLES OF THE BALL

How do we look?"

Zoop! Zoop! That was the sound of me doing a double take. Because the last thing I expected when I walked into the cabin after a long day of work was to see Mom and Georgia all dressed up for a party! Mom even smelled like perfume. I still smelled like roasted coffee—and Gavin's feet.

"What's going on?" I asked.

"Tonight is the Green Banks Gala!" said Mom. "And Mr. Pincus came by to give us three tickets. Wasn't that nice of him?"

Of course, I knew all about the Green Banks Gala. I'd been hearing about it all summer. It was legendary. It was a huge party that happened near

the end of every season in the main dining hall.
Mr. Pincus always had it catered from outside so
all the Green Banks workers could attend. But
I never thought in a million years they would
include *us*. I still thought of us Khatchadorians as
outcasts, me especially. Whenever I think about a
rich-people party, I picture myself outside with my
face pressed up against a window, like a hungry
orphan.

Mom did a little spin in the middle of the
kitchen. She had her hair down, which she almost
never does. And I really liked her dress. Blue is my
favorite color.

"You look like Cinderella!" I said.

"So what does that make *me*?" said Georgia. "The ugly stepsister?"

"Lose the 'tude," I said. "You look nice too." And she actually did. My sister is not exactly what you'd call a *fashionista*. Most days, she just ties her hair in a ponytail and runs around in jeans and a T-shirt. But when she actually works at it, she looks—I can't say *pretty*. That would be weird. So let's just go with *sort of cute.*

"Where did you guys get those fancy duds?" I asked.

"Rafe," said Mom. "You should know that a lady never travels without a dress. You never know what's going to come up!" That's my mom. Ready for anything. Even in a hobbit house in the middle of the woods.

When I went into the bedroom, I couldn't believe it. Lying on the top of my bunk were a pair of dark slacks and a clean white long-sleeved shirt. Mom poked her head in.

"You packed these too?" I asked.

"Guilty!" said Mom. "Now hurry up and take your shower—and let's get moving!"

"If we miss the appetizers, I'll *murder* you!" shouted Georgia from the living room. So much for sort of cute.

CHAPTER 46

PARTY FAVORS

A little observation: sometimes you don't always appreciate the nice parts of the place you work because you see them every day. (Or because you're usually staring down into a clam pit or a scrub bucket.) So when Mom and Georgia and I walked into the Green Banks Dining Hall that night, we were blown away!

It was the first time I noticed that the chandeliers were made of moose antlers, and they were all lit up with a golden glow. The floor was solid wood and it glowed right back. The place was filled with people I recognized—but instead of everyday polo shirts and khaki shorts, they were wearing sharp-looking sport coats and fancy party gowns.

The Green Banks String Quartet was playing on a little stage at one end of the dining hall—and they sounded pretty great. At the other end of the room was a long table covered in white tablecloths. On top was a long line of those big silver food warmers with little blue flames underneath. There were about *twenty* of them! I could already smell the pheasant!

"Welcome, Khatchadorians!"

It was our host, Mr. Pincus. He was still wearing his lumberjack shirt, but he had a black velvet jacket pulled over it. And it looked like he might even have trimmed his beard a little.

"Mr. Pincus!" said Mom. "Thank you so much for inviting us. Everything is so beautiful!" She looked down at us. "Isn't it, kids?"

"Absolutely!" I said. "Really great!"

"Definitely!" said Georgia. "Are there any appetizers?"

Mr. Pincus laughed and bent down to Georgia's eye level. "See that table over there?" He nodded toward a round table in the middle of the room. "It's *loaded* with them!"

"Wow! Thank you!" said Georgia. She was off like a shot.

"Enjoy!" said Mr. Pincus. "And Rafe?" He looked me in the eye with a fake-serious expression.

"Yes, sir?"

"No driving backward tonight!" Then he started laughing again and walked off to greet more guests—slapping backs, shaking hands, giving bear hugs.

I was glad Mr. Pincus was able to joke about my most embarrassing moment. For me, the shame still lingered. Mom tapped me on the arm.

"Keep an eye on your sister," she said. "I should go mingle."

As Mom went off to work the room, I walked over to the kiddie bar, which was a long table covered with every kind of beverage you can imagine: Gunkledunk Spring Water, Sprucy Juice in every fruit flavor under the sun, and over on the end—in huge liter-size bottles—a stockpile of Zoom soda!

Mr. Pincus sure knew how to throw a party. I took a plastic cup and poured myself a tall one. As I leaned back to enjoy the scene, I felt something big and sweaty next to me. I looked up.

"Hey, Lemur Lad, how's it going?" It was Gavin, wearing a suit that almost fit. His hair was combed like it was senior portrait day, and his sneer-smile was more smiley than usual. Standing next to him was a tall, skinny girl with red hair. This must be his Cinder date! I could tell right away she was a fellow Zoom fan. She'd filled her glass to the brim with Orange Blast flavor, which was my favorite too. She gave me a little wave like she'd seen me before and said, "Hi," in a whiny little voice. I recognized it right away.

Well, hello there...*Congo Kim*!

CHAPTER 47

PARTNERS IN CRIME

I hustled over to Georgia, who was standing at the appetizer table, feasting on mini-quiches. Her cheeks were so stuffed she looked like one of the chipmunks in Mom's painting.

"Wipe your mouth!" I said. There were quiche crumbs all over her face.

"These appetizers are the *best*!" she said. "Try the lobster pockets!"

"Forget that!" I said. "Look who's here!"

I pointed across the room, where Gavin and the skinny girl were chatting.

"Wait. Is that Congo Kim?" said Georgia.

"Yes!" I said. "It's her! And I bet she has the whole inside scoop on Congo Park and the lion and everything!"

"We need to pump her for info—*pronto*!" said Georgia.

"You read my mind," I said.

Georgia picked up a napkin and cleaned herself off. She was focused like a laser now. "What's she doing with Gavin?" she asked.

"He's her date," I said. "They found each other on Cinder."

"Ewww!" said Georgia. "I guess there's no accounting for taste."

"So what's the plan?" I said.

"I'll go say hello. Then I'll ask her if she wants to join me in the ladies' room."

"What if she says no?"

"Girls never say no to the ladies' room. We have a pact."

"Then what will you...?"

Too late. Georgia was already gone. I lost her in the crowd as more people moved in on the appetizer table. It was turning into a real feeding frenzy. I reached for a lobster pocket. Suddenly, I felt a firm hand on my shoulder. I knew it. *Time's up.* Somebody was about to toss me out.

"Rafe? It *is* Rafe, correct?"

Oh no! Of all people! It was Mr. Malarkey! Mega-billionaire. And the owner of one sunk SUV, compliments of me. I turned bright red.

"Yes, sir. Rafe Khatchadorian. Really sorry about your car, sir."

"Not your fault," said Mr. Malarkey. "Serves me right for not doing the job myself. Anyway, it'll be a nice tax write-off."

Not sure what that last part meant, but it made me feel a little better.

"Actually, Rafe," Mr. Malarkey went on, "I wanted to *thank* you."

"*Thank* me?" Now I was totally confused.

"That job you did scraping my boat hull was top-notch. Really cut down on our frictional resistance. I think it helped us bring home the trophy!"

"The trophy?" I said. "You mean you won the regatta?"

"By a nautical mile!" he said. "See for yourself!" He pointed up to a glass case on the wall. There was a little spotlight on the regatta trophy, with a nice big color photo of the *Buckaroo* alongside.

I didn't know what to say.

"Glad I could help" was all that came out.

"Maybe next year, you'll join the crew!" said Mr. Malarkey, giving me a big slap on the back. "Meantime, you need anything, you let me know!" Then he walked off to gloat among the losing captains.

"We're in!" Georgia was back.

"In where?" I said.

"You were right. Congo Kim knows the whole layout. She says the lion tamer is a real sleazebag, and she wants to save the lion too—just like us!"

"Nice work," I said. We did a little sibling fist bump.

I looked across the crowded room and caught Congo Kim's eye. I raised my glass of Zoom soda in her direction. She raised hers back.

As the old country song says, it's good to have friends in low places.

CHAPTER 48

NiGHT CREATURES

By ten o'clock, I was exhausted. And I wasn't
the only one. Georgia was slumped in a chair
with a plateful of tiny pies on her lap. I saw her
eyes start to glaze over. We had feasted like royalty,
and now we both had a bad case of the grogs.

"You guys ready for bed?" said Mom.

I could tell she was partied out too—even
though it looked like she'd had a really great time.

"What a terrific night!" she said, which made
me feel really good. After everything I'd put Mom
through that summer, it was nice to see her cut
loose. I even saw her waltzing with Mr. Pincus!

Everybody at the gala said it had been a huge
success, maybe the best year ever! People even
said the coffee had a little extra kick. (Um, no

comment.) Mom had spent some time talking to Mr. Malarkey, and how's *this* for a coincidence? Before he became a billionaire, Mr. M. was an art student too!

By the time Mom and Georgia and I headed out the door, the Green Banks String Quartet had been replaced by a DJ named Wolfpit. The beat was so loud it rattled the antlers in the chandeliers. My final snapshot image of the party before we closed the door behind us was this: Gavin doing the floss dance while Congo Kim turned bright red—and it wasn't from the sunburn.

As we walked back to the cabin, we could hear crickets in the bushes and bullfrogs in the pond, along with the *thump-thump-thump* of dance music fading behind us. Mom probably should have brought along some walking shoes because her party heels were definitely not made for off-roading. But the night air was so sweet and cool, she didn't seem to mind.

It wasn't long before we saw the porch light of our little hobbit home glowing through the trees. And then we heard the sound—a low rumbling from across the lake. Georgia and I looked at each other.

"What was that?" Mom said. She stopped to look around.

"What was *what*?" I said.

"Sorry," said Georgia, "I burped."

Nice save.

"You really need to lay off the mini-quiches," I said, a little louder than I needed to. We all started walking toward the cabin again.

"Your brother's right!" Mom laughed. "You sound like some kind of wild animal!"

As soon as Georgia flopped onto her bunk,

she started texting Congo Kim. The wireless connection was so slow they could have done better with smoke signals. But eventually, they got things arranged. Georgia held her phone down over her bunk to show me Congo Kim's last text:

This girl was not messing around. I didn't know what she had in mind, but I liked her style.

CHAPTER 49

BACK TO THE SCENE OF THE CRIME

The next day was Sunday—my day off. And it wasn't hard to talk Mom into another trip to her favorite painting spot. I knew she'd been wanting to add more foliage to her creek painting. As if it weren't beautiful enough already!

"Are you sure you kids don't mind?" she asked.

"No problemo!" I said. "We'll just hang out at Congo Park. We've got lots to do there." Of course, Mom didn't catch my hidden meaning. We were definitely going to do *something* at Congo Park. We just didn't know what. Yet.

I told Mom we needed to stop by the tool garage because I'd forgotten to plug in Gavin's chain saw charger. When I came out, she didn't even notice I had stashed a big burglary tool down the leg of my jeans.

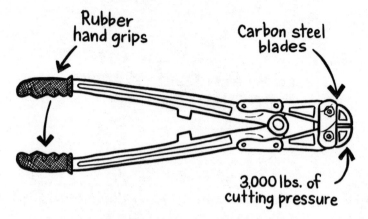

Rubber hand grips

Carbon steel blades

3,000 lbs. of cutting pressure

Recommended by convicts everywhere

For the whole ride, Georgia was more fidgety than usual. I held my hand against my pant leg so the bolt cutter wouldn't rattle. I felt like a criminal—and I hadn't even stolen anything yet. Except a bolt cutter.

"Let's hear some music!" said Georgia.

Mom cranked up the radio. What are the odds? It was Katy Perry!

Louder, louder than a lion! 'Cause I am a champion, and you're gonna hear me roooarroar!

CHAPTER 50

MASTERMINDLESS

After we paid our admission and got our hands stamped, we headed straight for the CongoCoaster. Congo Kim stood by the track in her African robe, waving a flyer at anybody who came close. She looked up when she saw us.

"Hi, guys," she said in her whiny voice. "Did you bring it?"

Georgia tapped my leg. "Got it," she said.

"Good. Now we just have to wait for Gavin."

Gavin?! Time out. I didn't count on Gavin being part of the plot. Even on my day off, I couldn't seem to shake this guy. He kept turning up everywhere I went—*like a bad penny*, as Grandma Dotty would say. How did we know he wouldn't rat us out? I

wasn't exactly his favorite person, so why would he
want to help?

Just then, the CongoCoaster came around
the bend and we heard a loud howl, like the
Abominable Snowman with his toe caught in a
bear trap.

"AROOOOOGGGH!"

As the coaster cars flew by, we could see Gavin
in the very front seat—about three feet taller than
the kids behind him. His hands were gripping the
bar in front of him, and his eyes were open wide.

"AROOOOOGGGH!"

"He told me he's been riding that thing since he was five," Congo Kim shouted over the clatter. No wonder Gavin was a little strange in the head. All those years on the CongoCoaster probably loosened a few screws.

When the ride came to a stop, it made a grinding noise so loud it hurt my ears. Gavin unbuckled his seat belt and stretched himself out of the coaster car. He looked like a lawn chair unfolding.

Gavin smile-sneered at Georgia and me. Then he reached over to hold Congo Kim's hand. She shooed him away like a horsefly.

"Quit it!" she whispered. "I'm on duty!"

"Right. My bad," said Gavin. He looked down at me and then glanced around as if he was afraid somebody was listening.

"Did you bring it?" he mumbled—like the world's most obvious spy.

I tapped my leg. I still wasn't sure I was okay with Gavin being involved.

"Excellent," he said. "Let's go!"

Congo Kim led the way down the hill. Then she took us on a quick detour off to the side, behind a giant Jungle Show sign. There was a little dirt trail just one person wide that went behind the clearing where the performance happened. I could tell Georgia was keeping her eyes peeled for poison ivy. Where the trail ended, a chain link fence started. We followed it along for about twenty yards. Then we stopped. Inside the fence was a wide area with bare dirt and scrubby grass that looked very familiar. Georgia elbowed me in the ribs.

Sure enough, this was it—the place where we'd first seen the lion a few nights ago. And there was the lion cage. Right in plain sight! In daylight, the place looked even tackier—and the cage looked even smaller. We all huddled down between the bushes and the fence. We could see the lion pacing around inside his cage—or trying to, anyway. Not a lot of room in there to take more than a couple of steps.

"So what's the plan?" I asked. Congo Kim looked up at Gavin. Uh-oh. That meant Gavin was in charge of the operation. He rubbed his hands together and lowered his head to our level, trying not to stand out like a sore thumb.

"First we cut a hole in the fence," he said, "then we cut the lock off the cage door!"

"*Then* what?" I asked.

"Then we set the lion free in the woods—back to nature, where he belongs!"

I had heard plenty of harebrained schemes in my time. In fact, as you probably know, I've had a few myself. But this one was a *doozy*! I had a whole list of things I thought the bolt cutter might be for—like breaking into an office or cracking open a file cabinet to find some incriminating photos. Cutting the padlock off a lion cage—*and letting a lion loose*—was definitely NOT on the list!

"An African lion can't survive in the woods!" I said. "He's a *savannah* animal!"

"Woods, jungle, savannah—what's the difference?" said Gavin. "He'll roam. He'll prowl. He'll hunt for game!"

"He's never hunted in his life!" I said. "They bring him meat in a bucket. He'd starve in a week!"

"This was the big plan?" Georgia whispered to Congo Kim. "A lion jailbreak?"

I could tell from the look on Congo Kim's face that she hadn't really thought the mission through. I guess she'd just trusted Gavin, who was obviously trying to impress her with his manliness. Big mistake. I'm sure she was regretting that swipe on Cinder right now.

I looked at Gavin. Even though he was still technically my boss, I was about to say, "You're nuts!!" But then we heard another voice.

"Hey, you kids can't be back here!" It was a

Congo Park security guard, wearing a pith helmet and carrying a huge walkie-talkie. We all looked at Congo Kim.

"I was just giving my friends a behind-the-scenes tour," she said.

"Well, this ain't on the tour," said the guard. "If you want to see the show, it's that way." He pointed toward the clearing.

Whew!

Personally, I had never been so happy to see a plan foiled in my life! I had images of the poor lion wandering around the woods looking for people to hand him buckets of meat. There would be a lot of heart attacks, and we'd be responsible.

Not that I didn't want to help him. His life right now was just...sad. Not pretty. Not dignified. He deserved better. But I was starting to believe that maybe living in a cage and doing tricks for tourists was all he had in store for him.

What could a bunch of kids do?

"We'll think of something," said Congo Kim. "Just act cool."

Easy for you to say, I thought. *You're not the one with a bolt cutter down your pants.*

We walked back to the show area. Congo Kim flashed her name tag in front of the gawky kid at the entrance and we got seats right up front. We were so close we could smell the sawdust.

The Sunday crowd was *way* bigger than it was in the middle of the week. Every seat was filled. A lady in a big orange muumuu sat right behind us. She filled *two* seats.

"Ladies and gentlemen!"

Yep. We had to sit through the whole corny introduction again, static and all.

But I won't put you through it. In a nutshell, Monsieur DeFarge came out just like before. Started cracking his whip. The lion popped out of the tunnel. And so forth and so on…

The act went on exactly the same as the first time. From where we were sitting, the whip cracks were even louder. If I were a lion, that sound would get on my last nerve!

The lion hopped from platform to platform. The audience clapped—but kind of like golf clapping. Polite, but nothing to get your blood stirring.

Until…the lion tamer picked up the giant ring!

A buzz went through the crowd. Everybody

knew this was the big moment. He pulled out the lighter. He flicked on the flame. He lit the ring. The fire raced around the circle. We could see the little waves of heat coming off it. From far away, this part of the act looked pretty cool. From up close, it looked totally *insane!*

The lion tamer held up the ring, just like last time. He cracked the whip once! Twice! Three times! The lion gathered his strength. He tightened his haunches.

"Hey, lion! Look over here!"

It was the muumuu lady behind us, holding her phone out in front of her. At the very second the lion made his leap, she clicked! She obviously forgot to turn off the flash because we could see a little white burst reflected in the lion's eyes.

It must have thrown a wrench in his timing. From there on, I felt like I was watching a train wreck in slow motion.

When the lion jumped through the ring, the top of his mane brushed the bottom of the flames. And when he landed on the other side, his hair tips were smoking!

The lion tamer shouted a swear word in French and reached behind a fake palm tree. He pulled out a fire extinguisher and sprayed white foam all over the lion's head, until it looked like a Frosted Congo Cone. Then he yelled at the lion—like it was *his* fault for spoiling the big finale.

Some of the kids laughed like they thought this was all part of the act. But the four of us—me, Georgia, Gavin, and Congo Kim—just stared at the ring. It couldn't be good for the lion to be covered in chemicals like that—he kept trying to paw the white goop off his face and lick it away. But the lion tamer didn't seem to care. He was still ranting and raving in French, trying to prod the poor lion back onto a platform, even though his fur was still singed and smoking.

I couldn't tell if the lion was hurt, but he'd probably jumped through that flaming hoop thousands of times. Judging by the quick way the ringmaster whipped out the fire extinguisher, I doubted this was the first time the lion had caught on fire.

Georgia turned beet red and stood up. "We've got to *do* something!" she said. This time, I was way ahead of her. I took out my phone and snapped a photo of the whole pathetic, foamy scene.

Exhibit A

By the time the lion tamer finished his tantrum, I had already pressed Send.

CHAPTER 51

HOT PURSUIT!

Four hours later…the reply arrived. In a pretty
dramatic way.

A bright green Jeep blasted through the main
entrance. Following right behind was a dark green
pickup truck. On the door, in bright gold letters, it
said COUNTY WILDLIFE ENFORCEMENT. The cavalry was
here!

Dr. Deerwin pulled the Jeep to a stop in the
middle of the Congo Park compound. I could see
Penelope leaning out the passenger-side window,
braids flying. The pickup screeched to a stop right
alongside.

The four of us had been killing time in the food
court nearby. I took the bolt cutter out of my pants

and handed it over to Gavin. No need for it now. I felt a weight lifted off me. (About two pounds, probably.) Now *real* help was here!

"Rafe! Jump in!" shouted Dr. Deerwin, leaning out of the driver's-side window. I ran over and hopped into the backseat of the Jeep. Georgia, Gavin, and Congo Kim crowded into the crew cab of the pickup truck. As I buckled my seat belt, Penelope popped her head around the front seat.

"We g-g-got here as f-f-fast as we c-c-could!"

"I'm really glad you're here!" I said. That was what you call a loaded statement. Because it was true in so many ways. My heart was pounding like a drum.

"Rafe! Focus!" Dr. Deerwin shouted. "Which way?"

"Follow that trail!" I said. I pointed down the hill toward the Jungle Show. She gunned the Jeep. It was like being in a real-life adventure movie! We bounced down the trail until we came to the big Jungle Show sign.

"Stop here!" I yelled. Dr. Deerwin pulled the Jeep off to the side. The pickup pulled off behind her. I saw two super-buff wildlife officers pop out of the truck. They had green uniforms, leather gloves, and utility belts with all kinds of cool tools and weapons.

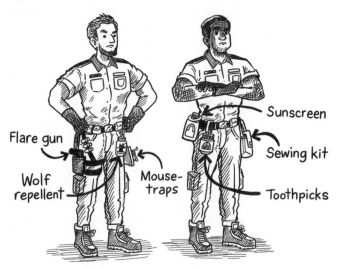

Flare gun

Wolf repellent

Mouse-traps

Sunscreen

Sewing kit

Toothpicks

Georgia, Gavin, and Congo piled out after them. Georgia's eyes were as wide as saucers.

"This is Biff. And this is Bo," Dr. Deerwin said. "They're wildlife officers."

"I'm Rafe," I said. Biff and Bo nodded. No smiles. All business. The strong, silent type.

I led the way down the narrow trail until we got to the chain link fence. The lion was back in his cage. He still had foam on his mane. Dr. Deerwin took one look at the big lion and the tiny cage and got really quiet. I saw the veins in her neck start to pound.

"This is unbelievable!" said Dr. Deerwin.

"This is d-d-disgusting!" said Penelope.

"This is *illegal*," said Biff.

Bo stuck his glove under the chain link fence and yanked up on it to make a big opening. It was like he was lifting tissue paper. The Human Bolt Cutter.

We all crawled under the fence. Biff and Bo headed for a trailer on the other side of the cage. Dr. Deerwin waved her hand at us.

"Stay back, kids!" she said.

Penelope looked across the yard to the cage and locked eyes with the lion.

"Hang on, baby," she whispered. "We *got* you!"

All of a sudden, the trailer door jerked open and Monsieur DeFarge popped out. He was still wearing his black leather boots and safari pants. But on top, he just had a sleeveless T-shirt. His arms and shoulders were all hairy. He was holding a sandwich and there was some mayo on his moustache.

"Que se passe-t-il!" he shouted, which must be French for "What the heck is going on?!"

Biff and Bo held up their badges and started asking for things like animal exhibition licenses, employment visas, and all kinds of legal stuff. DeFarge acted all friendly and cooperative. Then, as he turned to go back into his trailer for the paperwork, he started to make a run for it! He was headed for the woods!

Bo and Biff just looked at each other. I thought they might pull out a lasso or something, but they just walked after DeFarge, caught up to him, and lifted him up.

Game over, *Monsieur*!

CHAPTER 52

JUNGLE JUSTICE

We all hiked back up the trail and then rode in the vehicles to the main part of the park. When kids and parents saw DeFarge in handcuffs, they all whipped out their cell phones to record the big arrest.

GunkleDunk Times

Local Lion Tamer
Deported!
"So long, Sleazebag!"
says police chief

When I got out of the Jeep, I noticed that there was a huge folding cage strapped to the back— along with some thick padding.

"Think he'll fit?" asked Dr. Deerwin.

"You mean you're taking him away?"

"Your lion belongs someplace where people will take care of him. He's done jumping through hoops."

Your lion. I liked the sound of that.

"We're b-b-bringing him b-b-back to B-BushyTail!" said Penelope.

"All we need is some paperwork from Biff and Bo and we're good to go," said Dr. Deerwin.

Congo Kim clapped her hands together like she'd just witnessed a miracle. I think it was the first time I'd ever seen her smile. Gavin pumped his fist in the air, like it was all his doing—which in a roundabout way, it was. If he hadn't been trying so hard to impress his new girlfriend, he wouldn't have been so determined to hatch a rescue plan for the lion. It turned out to be a terrible plan, but it was what got Georgia and me back to Congo Park. And if we hadn't been at

Congo Park that very day, we wouldn't have seen the catastrophe—which was what made the *real* rescue happen. So in a crazy way, love saved the day!

While Penelope went to pick up the papers from Biff and Bo, Dr. Deerwin walked over to where I was standing with Gavin and Congo Kim.

"Rafe, you know you helped to save your lion's life, right?"

"It was a team effort," I said.

Dr. Deerwin leaned down to my level. "Don't quote me on this," she said, "but if you're interested, I think I might be able to get you back your old job at BushyTail."

I felt a wave of excitement shoot through me. My head was spinning so fast I could only get one word out.

"YESSSS!"

"Let me talk to Mr. Pincus," she said. "Both of them."

I was in a daze. But a really happy one. I couldn't wait to tell Mom! I couldn't wait to sleep in my own moth-free bed again! Congo Kim gave me a hug. Gavin gave me a bone-crusher handshake.

"Take care, Lemur Lad," he said. And I think he
actually meant it.

All in all, it had been quite a day. And a big
inspiration for me. Maybe I'd do my animal report
on *lions*!

CHAPTER 53

TALL ORDER

On my first day back at BushyTail, I didn't even know where to start!

Mr. Pincus handed me a bucket and a shovel.

"Start with the chimps," he said.

Hard to believe, but I'd never been so happy to clean up a smelly, icky mess in my life! I think the chimps were actually glad to see me because there was hardly any poop-tossing at all. Mostly they just screeched and rocked back and forth and picked bugs off each other for snacks. Home sweet home!

After I emptied a few bucketfuls of chimp slop, I headed over to the lemur enclosure. Naturally, I had mixed feelings. After all, this was the conspiracy that got me into so much trouble in the first place. On the other hand, I was the one who left the gate unlocked—and I guess I couldn't blame the lemurs for running off. I probably would've done the same thing in their situation.

Loretta was the first one into my lap. Yep, I knew them all by name now. It's like a classroom full of new kids, I guess. On your first day, it's hard to tell everybody apart. But then you start noticing that Larry's ears are a little uneven, and that Lily's tail is bent at the end, and that Lamar always eats the head of the cricket first. Pretty soon they're as different as Flip Savage and Miller the Killer.

The lemurs went through their breakfast pail in no time. I'd never seen dead insects bring so much joy. I was playing with one of the cute little lemur babies when I heard a familiar sound.

Beep, beep!

It was the horn on the BushyTail golf cart—and guess who was at the wheel?

Penelope!

"T-Time to f-f-feed the g-giraffes!" she yelled.
Music to my ears.

I tossed the last cricket to Loretta for old times'
sake, and then I went through the gate toward the
golf cart. I was pretty excited. I couldn't wait to see
Cain and Abel.

Okay. I know what you're thinking.

Right now, you're wondering if I'd learned my
lesson. Did I forget to close the lemur gate again?
Fair question. But you can stop wondering. I not
only closed the gate and lowered the latch—I
tied it tight with a knot called a buntline hitch. I
learned that one from Mr. Malarkey. And there was
no way little lemur paws could untie it!

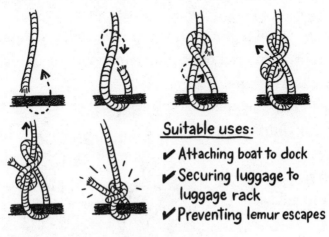

Suitable uses:
✔ Attaching boat to dock
✔ Securing luggage to
   luggage rack
✔ Preventing lemur escapes

As soon as I hopped into the golf cart next to Penelope, I could smell the aroma of fresh alfalfa from the bin in back.

"S-S-Strap in!" she said.

I fastened my seat belt. She jammed her foot down on the accelerator—and we were *off*!

"G-G-Glad you're b-back," said Penelope as the cart whined its way up a hill.

"Me too," I said.

"G-Guess who's been d-doing all your w-work while you were g-gone?"

"You?" I said.

"M-Me! And those ch-chimps really s-s-stink!" she said, pinching her nose.

I asked Penelope to take the long way around so we could make a few stops along the way. I checked in on Eight Ball the turtle (still swimming in circles). I tested my chameleon-spotting skills at the lizard cage. I paused to pet some new capybara pups and gave the boa constrictor a pat on both heads.

Welcome home!

Ditto!

But Penelope and I were both itching to get to the giraffes, so I cut my reunion tour short. In a few minutes, we pulled up at the stockade fence outside the giraffe enclosure.

"How's Abel doing?" I asked as we opened the alfalfa bin.

"Sh-She's about f-f-fifteen months along," said Penelope. "So f-far, so g-good."

Patient name: Abel
Species: Giraffa
Mate: Cain
Age: 8
Height: 240 inches
Weight gain since last visit: 150 lbs.
Due date: Anytime now!

We walked through the gate holding about a bushel of alfalfa each. As soon as Cain saw us, he slow-walked over and started munching big bunches from my hand. Abel was standing over by the fence, looking kind of out of it. Since the last time I saw her, she was looking even puffier, and she was moving verrrry slowwwwly. It took her a whole minute to walk over, and when she got to us, she barely nibbled. Penelope ran her palm over Abel's soft nose.

"Not hungry, honey?" she asked.

All of a sudden, a trickle of water splashed into the dirt.

"Abel, c'mon!" I laughed. "You couldn't wait to pee?"

Penelope ran her hand along Abel's side and did a quick check under her tail.

"She's n-n-not p-peeing, Rafe!" said Penelope. "Her w-water just b-broke!"

Now, I admit I'm still pretty much in the dark when it comes to the birds and the bees. I'm not even sure how tadpoles happen. But I've watched enough TV to guess that when you're expecting a baby, this water-breaking thing is a pretty big deal.

Penelope pulled out her phone and tapped once.

"Hey, M-M-M-Mom!" she said. "It's t-t-time!"

CHAPTER 54

SPECIAL DELIVERY!

P ush, Abel, push!"
Dr. Deerwin stood behind Abel, wearing blue rubber gloves that went way up past her elbows. Mr. Pincus paced back and forth like a dad in a waiting room, grunting the whole time. Cain—the *actual* dad—watched from a distance, munching on a pile of alfalfa. I guess he was satisfied to let nature take its course. Not much he could do to help at this point, anyway.

I stood with Dr. Deerwin and Penelope, staring at the part of Abel where all the action was supposed to happen. We'd been waiting for an hour.

And waiting...

All of a sudden, we saw two perfect little hooves

pop out! Then a pair of skinny pinkish legs! But just the lower halves.

Then everything kind of stopped.

A minute went by. Then two minutes.

I knew exactly how long because Penelope was calling out the time and recording every stat in her notebook. Once in a while, Abel shifted her legs and swung her long neck around to check on the progress herself. It was hard to tell what she was thinking behind those big brown eyes. But I could tell that Dr. Deerwin was getting nervous.

"M-Mom, is everything o-k-kay?" said Penelope.

"Just waiting for the head to show up," said Dr. Deerwin. She patted Abel on the side. "C'mon, Abel, you need to *push*!"

Another minute went by. Then another. The little hooves and legs were just hanging out there like parts of a toy animal.

Dr. Deerwin stepped up onto a short ladder so that her head was even with the baby's legs. She tugged her gloves tight and wiggled her fingers.

"I need to go in!" she said.

In? Did she mean...?

Yep. That's what she meant. Prepare yourself.

Slowly, carefully, gently, Dr. Deerwin slid her hands up *inside* Abel, right alongside the baby's legs. A few seconds went by as she felt her way.

"I can feel the head!" she shouted. "But it's stuck!"

Mr. Pincus started pacing faster and grunting louder.

In crisis situations, my mind sometimes wanders. I remember thinking this is probably why vet school takes so long. The first couple of years, you're probably just sitting in class memorizing body parts.

But sooner or later, if you really, really love animals, you're going to have to get your hands dirty. Like getting elbow-deep in the back end of a two-story giraffe. Dr. Deerwin turned her head to look at me.

"Rafe! Get over here, you're just the right height."

For what? I was afraid to ask.

"Grab some gloves!"

Penelope tossed me a pair of thin blue

gloves—not as long as Dr. Deerwin's, but pretty professional-looking just the same.

Dr. Deerwin shifted her hands inside Abel. "I need you to grab just above the hooves!" she said.

Was this really *happening*?? Was I, Rafe Khatchadorian, really going to help to pull a calf out of a giraffe? If only Mr. Manta could see me now! This was a long way from staring at tadpoles.

I wrapped my hands around the baby's ankles. I could feel the bones through the thin fur. Everything was slick with some kind of clear mucus. In a normal situation, it might have felt gross. But right now, all I cared about was helping Abel and her baby—and if I had to deal with a little slime along the way, so what!

"Now pull!" said Dr. Deerwin. "Slowly!" I tightened my grip and leaned back, petrified I was going to break the baby somehow. No luck. The legs barely moved an inch.

Dr. Deerwin pressed in closer against Abel and shifted her arms again.

"Ready, Rafe?" she said. "On three, pull hard."

"Got it!" I said.
"One! Two! *Three!*"

I leaned back again. It was like trying to yank a cork out of a bottle—if the bottle weighed a ton and a half and the cork had a mind of its own. But then...

I felt the legs start to slide back with me—a couple of inches at a time.

"The head's free!" shouted Dr. Deerwin. Sure enough, when she pulled her arms out, a miniature giraffe head started to peek out too!

"It's okay, Rafe!" called Dr. Deerwin. "Let Abel take it from here!"

I let go and stood back. Abel shifted her legs again. She raised her head. Her tail curled to the side. Then, in one final heave, the calf slid out and fell hoof-first onto the grass. It was about a five-foot drop! The calf was kind of gray and splotchy all over, and it was covered with a layer of goop.

Amazing! A few seconds ago, it was just a pair of hooves sticking out. Now it was a living, breathing...

But wait. Something was wrong!

The calf was lying still on the grass. Not moving. Not *breathing*!

I reached out to shake the baby, but Dr. Deerwin held me back.

"Wait," she said. "Just wait."

The next minute was maybe the longest one of my life. Abel shifted her feet and swung her huge body around. She towered over the baby like a skyscraper. Then she lowered her long neck and nudged the baby with her snout.

Still nothing. Not good!

Mr. Pincus stopped grunting and stood very still.

Then Abel started flicking her long tongue all

around the baby's face and nose, licking off the goop like it was ice cream. (Sorry. I have to tell it like it was.)

All of a sudden, the calf gave a little kick. Then a snort! It tucked its legs under its belly and raised its neck straight up. It looked at Abel. Then I swear it looked right at me!

Do I smell alfalfa?

"It's a girl!" said Dr. Deerwin.

Welcome to the world, little lady!

Mr. Pincus started grunting again—happy grunts now!

Penelope wrapped her arms around Abel's neck. "Congratulations," she said. "You're a *mother*!"

Dr. Deerwin yanked off her messy gloves and dropped them on the grass.

I did the same. She walked over to me. At first, I thought she was going to shake my hand—as a fellow giraffe deliverer. Instead, she picked me up off the ground and gave me one of the biggest hugs of my life!

But the best was yet to come...

CHAPTER 55

THE HEAT OF THE MOMENT

You d-d-did it!"

Penelope ran over and gave me a big hug too!

"We *all* did it," I said. "Especially Abel!" I was so relieved and excited. Before I could even think about what I was doing…it happened.

I kissed Penelope on the cheek.

As soon as I did it, I felt like my head was going to explode with embarrassment. My whole face was burning. I turned as pink as a flamingo.

"Sorry, sorry!" I said. "I got carried away!"

Penelope laughed. "It's okay, Rafe," she said. Then she kissed *me* on the cheek. "Actually, it was *perfect*!"

"Hey!" I said. "Your voice! How come you're not stutt…?"

Penelope put her hand over my mouth. Her eyes were closed.

"Shhhh!" she said. "I'm picturing you as a dead cricket."

That was probably the nicest thing anyone ever said to me. But she wasn't done yet. Penelope took her phone out of her pocket and held it up. She tapped her video screen and pressed Play. And there it was! There *I* was!

Rated PG: Content May Not be Suitable for Young Children!

She had recorded the whole giraffe birth in living color!

Pretty great ending, right?

But I wasn't out of the woods yet.

Because I *still* hadn't started my animal report!

CHAPTER 56

AFTERGLOW

One week later, I was sitting at the kitchen table watching Penelope's video on my laptop—for the 150th time.

"That is so *gross*!" said Georgia.

"That is so *beautiful*!" said Mom.

"Is that *The Bachelor*?" Said Grandma Dotty. (Grandma *really* needs new glasses.)

I had just spent seven days locked in my room trying to create the best animal report in Hills Village Middle School history. I hardly slept. I barely ate. I think I might have lost a few pounds. Once I decided what to write about, I put my whole heart and soul into it!

Can you guess what my topic was?

"Gestation & Birth
in the
African Giraffe"

by Rafe Khatchadorian, ARV
(Animal Rehab Volunteer)

My report was twenty pages, double-spaced,
with diagrams and bar graphs and temperature
charts and quotes from a leading local veterinarian
(guess who?). I topped the whole thing off with a
link to Penelope's video, which already had ten
million views on YouTube! And I handed it in to
Mr. Manta right under the wire.

Pretty impressive, if I do say so myself.

I closed my laptop and went back into my
bedroom. My dog, Junior, hopped onto the bed
with me, looking for some serious snuggle time.
He probably felt a little left out and jealous, and
I couldn't blame him. Don't get me wrong, Junior

is super cute, but it's hard to compete with a baby giraffe. While I scratched Junior's belly, I stared at the piece of paper taped to the wall over my dresser. I could still hardly believe it.

It was a certificate from Hills Village Middle School. In the middle, in big letters, it said *Science Requirement Fulfilled.* In the official space for the teacher's name it said *Manta, Ray.* And at the very bottom was something I thought I'd never live to see—especially coming from Mr. M.

A big, fat, juicy...

CHAPTER 57

ANIMAL OVERLOAD

At last, I was a free man! The cloud had lifted. My shame had ended! I planned to get reacquainted with my Wormhole game controller and log some serious tanning hours in my backyard. I had definitely earned some time off.

But just when I thought I was done...

Rrrinnggggg!

It was the home phone. Georgia picked it up.

"Rafe!" she yelled. "It's for you!"

I picked up the handset in the hallway.

"Hello?"

"I need help!"

It was Mr. Pincus—the farty one. And he sounded a little crazed. Apparently, the giraffe video had stirred a lot of interest in BushyTail. Too *much* interest! More animals were arriving every day—from everywhere! Too many to handle!

"Come tomorrow!" said Mr. Pincus. "Please!" Then he grunted and hung up.

Troll blasting and tanning would have to wait.

When Mom drove me to BushyTail the next morning, we could see the problem right away. Cars and trucks and vans were coming and going from every direction. The entrance area was crammed with boxes and crates and cages filled with every kind of abandoned pet you can imagine—unwanted iguanas, neglected guinea pigs, rejected gerbils. I even saw a couple of bowls of goldfish!

Mr. Pincus hurried over to the car.

"I'm running out of places to put them!" he said.

Mom looked over his shoulder at the main area past the entrance. She squinted. "Is that a *llama* over there?"

"A whole *family*!" said Mr. Pincus. "Just arrived from Peru last night!"

At that minute, another truck pulled up—the kind with a cab up front and a big trailer with wooden sides behind. The driver hopped out.

"Where do you want the walrus?" he said.

Mr. Pincus just grunted.

I have to admit, the rest of that day was a blur. I helped Mr. Pincus put up about a dozen temporary pens. I watered camels. I herded cats. I broke up a fight between an aardvark and an armadillo. It was exhausting!

When Mom picked me up that evening, I put my head back and slept for the whole ride home. As soon as I walked into the house, I just slumped down onto the sofa. Mom fixed me my favorite sandwich: cheese and baloney on white bread, with mayo and mustard. I sipped on a Zoom soda— nectar of the gods. That perked me up a little bit.

"Busy today?" she asked, even though my body language pretty much told the tale.

"Mr. Pincus is going nuts!" I said. "And he's making *me* nuts! He needs more fences, more pools, more gates—more *everything*!"

Supplies Needed!
- rope
- wire
- padlocks
- tarps
- straw
- feeding troughs
- slop buckets
- pool toys
- horn polish
- hoof scrapers
- fly paper
- air freshener

And that wasn't even counting all the new
kinds of animal food he had to buy. What do llamas
eat, anyway? Probably some kind of rare Peruvian
grass.

"How can he afford all that stuff?" Mom said.

"That's the thing," I said, "he can't. He needs
money, and a lot of it."

The truth was, I was thinking the unthinkable.
I was afraid Mr. Pincus would actually go out
of business. And where would that leave all the
animals he was taking care of? Obviously, nobody
else wanted them. BushyTail was kind of the last
stop for most of those guys. Just the idea of it made
me feel kind of sad and queasy.

Mom sat down on a chair across from me. She
leaned back and started twirling a finger through
her hair. She does that sometimes when her brain
is working. She didn't say anything for a while.
Finally, she looked up.

"Ever hear of a silent auction?" she said.

"You mean where a guy in suspenders talks
really fast and then whacks his hammer down?"

"Not exactly," said Mom. "A silent auction is

kind of like a big party, except that it's all about raising money for a good cause."

I liked the sound of that. BushyTail was a very good cause.

"Tell me more," I said. She really had my attention now.

"Well," said Mom, "in a silent auction, people donate all kinds of cool things and then the guests decide how much they're willing to pay for them. They write their bids down on a sheet of paper."

"That's the silent part?" I said.

"Right," said Mom. "Then at the end of the party, the highest bidders win the stuff and write a check to the cause."

It sounded a lot better than putting out a tip jar in the office, which was the only idea I had so far.

"You think that could work for BushyTail?" I asked.

"Worth a try!" said Mom.

Once again, Julia Khatchadorian had found a way to give me hope!

CHAPTER 58

POUNDING THE PAVEMENT

Turns out Georgia knew all about silent auctions. That's how her math team raised money for their matching polo shirts and monogrammed pocket protectors. So when Mom asked her to do up a flyer for the BushyTail event, she was all over it. And I have to admit, it came out pretty great.

Now all we had to do was distribute it. I voted for a mass emailing. Just press Send and done. But Georgia said we needed to pass the flyers out in person, one at a time. Old-school.

"We need to tape them up in every store window," she said. "And stick them on every windshield." She made a good point. We didn't have a lot of time. High visibility was the name of the game.

Of course, passing out flyers was just half the job. We also had to talk people into actually donating stuff for the auction. *Good* stuff. Stuff people would actually be willing to write big checks for. Fortunately, Georgia is pretty persuasive. Mostly, I just stood back and let her talk.

Naturally, Swifty's Diner was our first stop. Right away, Swifty agreed to donate a dozen pies, assorted flavors. Dolly at Hills Village Dry Cleaning came through with free pants-pressing for a year, plus unlimited wedding gown storage. Rico's Pest Control donated a termite inspection and a lawn grub treatment. Benny's Garage agreed to a free lube job and a set of all-terrain tires. We were definitely on a roll.

While Georgia and I made the rounds in town, Mom talked with Mr. Pincus about setting up the big event. Mr. Pincus wasn't exactly the party type. Like I said way back when I first met him, he was more comfortable around animals than people. But at this point he was so desperate that he was ready to try anything! Mom told him she could probably call in some favors from the PTA and the Rotary Club. And she thought the Elks Lodge might be willing to donate their tent.

By the end of the day, Georgia and I had papered Hills Village with flyers and lined up a bunch of pretty sweet donations. The question was: Would the auction bring in any big spenders who could save BushyTail from closing down?

We'd find out in exactly one week.

CHAPTER 59

SILENCE IS GOLDEN

In exactly one week...

The huge Elks Lodge tent was set up near BushyTail's main entrance. It looked a little rickety and it smelled like cigars, but beggars can't be choosers. Penelope and I had been blowing up balloons all morning and I have to say, the place was looking pretty festive. By noon, there was already a line of cars at the entrance—and before long, the tent was filled with people. Everybody was pretty excited. You could hear the chimps screeching and laughing in the distance, which added to the party atmosphere.

Inside the tent, there were rows of small tables displaying the prizes. Each table had a piece of paper with spaces for people to write their names

and how much they were willing to pay. The idea
was that if it was something you really wanted,
you would bid way more than anybody else to be
sure you got it!

Thanks to Georgia's flyer, everybody in Hills
Village had gotten the message about the big
event. A lot of my friends from school showed up—
including all my troll-busting video game buddies.
My friend Flip Savage, the funniest kid I know,
was telling animal jokes to anybody who would
listen.

Junior and Sulfur were getting acquainted the way dogs do: by sniffing each other's butts. Another great mystery of the animal kingdom. (And one I'd rather not think about.)

Georgia was collecting a ten-dollar admission charge at the front of the tent as people came in. (Kids under five free.) Every single one of her Math Mentor students showed up with their parents. That's loyalty. And the rest of her school math team volunteered to direct the parking—in perfect parallel rows. People were milling around inside the tent looking over the prizes and nudging each other aside to get to the good stuff. I saw a few scuffles, but nothing serious.

Over in one corner of the tent, Mom had a
little table of her own with some of her paintings,
including the one she did of the creek near Congo
Park. It was so beautiful I hated to see it go, but
if it could bring in a few bucks for BushyTail,
it would be worth the sacrifice. A couple of her
paintings already had some double-digit bids. But I
was counting on that creek painting to bring in the
big bucks!

Mr. Pincus was buzzing around the tent in the BushyTail golf cart. I guess he thought if he kept moving, he wouldn't have to talk to anybody. So far, so good.

All of a sudden I heard a big, booming voice.

"Rafe! Good to see you're back in the animal kingdom!"

I turned around. It was Mr. Pincus—the bearded one—all the way from Green Banks! He laughed and wrapped one of his big arms around my shoulders. I could smell the campfire smoke on his beard. It was really good to see him.

"Hi, Mr. Pincus," I said. "Mr. Pincus didn't tell me you were coming!"

"Wouldn't miss it for the world," he said. "Anything to assist creatures in need!"

He led me over to the Green Banks display table. He was donating a week in a lakefront cabin, plus two tickets to next year's Green Banks Gala! High-value items, for sure.

"I bet those will go for top dollar," I said.

"Hope so," said Mr. Pincus as he looked around. "This place could use some help!" He was so right.

Compared with Green Banks, BushyTail was a big step down. Instead of antler chandeliers, we were looking at bare bulbs hanging from cords. Instead of high-class appetizers, we were nibbling on peanuts and Grandma Dotty's toffee treats. Instead of the Green Banks Quartet, we were listening to Georgia's Spotify playlist—heavy on Lady Gaga.

When the other Mr. Pincus rolled up in his golf cart, I realized that I had never actually seen both brothers together in one place. They looked kind of like bookends. Just as they started grunting and talking in the middle of the tent, the Green Banks Mr. Pincus's pocket rang. He pulled out his phone.

"Ben!" he shouted when he heard the caller's voice. "Ben Malarkey!"

Mr. Malarkey? The billionaire from Green Banks? A blast from my recent past. Mr. Pincus listened for a few seconds and then lowered the phone.

"He's asking if we accept phone bids," he said to his brother.

The other Mr. Pincus grunted.

"Absolutely," Mr. Pincus said into the phone. "All bids are welcome!"

On the other side of the room, Mom was chatting with Mr. Manta. He was admiring the chipmunk details in her painting. Mr. Manta had donated one of his favorite *National Geographic* posters—the one with the grizzly bear. I was kind of hoping he'd donate his stuffed mongoose, but I guess that was too much to ask.

Mr. Pincus roamed around the tent holding his phone up. He was giving Mr. Malarkey a live FaceTime view of all the auction items. He passed by Mom, then by Dr. Deerwin's table. Dr. Deerwin and Penelope had arrived with a litter of kittens to auction off, along with a year's supply of vet visits and kitty litter. Mr. Pincus took a dramatic close-up of one of Swifty's pies, then got a group shot of the ladies from Hills Village Dry Cleaning. The crew from Benny's Garage posed with their heads sticking through the tires.

I walked through the crowd to check on Georgia, who was adding up the admission money. "How much did we take in so far?" I asked.

"Eighty people times ten dollars," she said. "You do the math."

Eight hundred dollars is not chicken feed. But it wasn't gonna go far at BushyTail. In fact, it would barely cover the cost of five bales of alfalfa. Cain and Abel could chew through that in a week.

I peeked at some of the bids on the tables. Fifty dollars here. A hundred dollars there. People were giving what they could, but it wasn't adding up to much, considering everything BushyTail needed.

Suddenly the bearded Mr. Pincus shouted, "We have a *phone* bid!"

The whole tent went quiet. Mr. Pincus held the phone close to his ear. He listened for a second or two.

"Got it," he said into the phone. "Are you sure?"

Mr. Pincus put down the phone and walked over to where Mom was standing. He swept his hand toward her table—and pointed to the creek painting.

"The bid is from Mr. Ben Malarkey of Malarkey

Media, for this wonderful woodland painting by Julia Khatchadorian!"

Mom started blushing. She was always a little shy about showing off her work.

"The bid," said Mr. Pincus in a loud voice, "is *one hundred thousand dollars!*"

The other Mr. Pincus started spinning around in his golf cart. People gasped. Then everybody started cheering. All the noise got Junior and Sulfur super excited. They started running around in circles. And somehow, they both got tangled in the support ropes around the main tent pole. Which didn't look that sturdy to start with.

Creeeeeak!

"Junior! Watch out!" I shouted.

Too late.

The pole started leaning to one side—and then started tipping over! A few ropes snapped! Then the whole tent kind of collapsed on top of the crowd in slow motion. It was like being under one of those blanket forts you build in your bedroom, except the whole town was underneath it. It wasn't so bad—besides the cigar smell. And the little kids thought it was really fun.

A couple of guys from the fire department
kept everybody calm and hoisted the tent pole up

enough for us to slip out. In a couple of minutes, we were all outside on the grass, breathing the fresh country air. From the outside, the tent looked like a giant melted marshmallow. I saw Georgia coming toward me clutching something to her chest. She had rescued the cash box. Not that eight hundred dollars was a big deal anymore!

We looked around for Mom, and there she was, standing by a corner of the tent holding on to her creek painting for dear life. Georgia and I ran over and gave her a big hug sandwich.

"We *told* you it was a great painting!" I said. Mom didn't say anything. She just squeezed us both really tight.

Mr. Pincus was circling what was left of the tent in his golf cart. I'd never seen him look happier. A hundred thousand dollars buys a lot of alfalfa!

Junior and Sulfur were running around like best buddies. It looked like the beginning of a beautiful friendship.

So, aside from the tent collapse, the day had gone really well.

It looked like BushyTail was saved!

CHAPTER 60

END OF THE TRAIL

S low down!" I said. "You don't have to drink it all in one gulp!"

It was the last hour of my last afternoon before I had to go back to school. Penelope and I were in the giraffe enclosure feeding the new baby. I was thinking that I'd never seen a summer go by so fast. A lot had happened since that fateful meeting with Mr. Manta.

I held up a big bottle while the calf sucked down formula. Oh, by the way—the baby had a name now. Her name was Jules, after my mom! It was Mr. Pincus's idea. In fact, he *insisted* on it.

Jules normally got milk directly from her mother, but Dr. Deerwin wanted to add some vitamin supplements to her diet, just in case.

That's where the bottle came in. I had to stand on a stool just to reach the calf's mouth. She was almost six feet tall already. Why couldn't *I* grow this fast? I guess I was lacking giraffe genes.

After Jules guzzled the whole bottle, Penelope and I put out a couple of bales of alfalfa for her parents. We locked the gate behind us—I double-checked like I always do now—and walked down the trail to the main compound, past the chimps and the lemurs and the llamas. We came to a brand-new fenced-in space, covered in tall green grass. At first, it looked totally empty. Suddenly, we heard a loud roar. We saw something moving in the distance.

And then...there he was! The lion! *My* lion!

He still wasn't used to walking on natural surfaces. He lifted his paws and sniffed the ground with every step, like he couldn't believe it was real. When he spotted us at the fence, he let out another roar—even louder this time. I'm no expert, but to me, he sounded proud and in charge. Like a king!

Beep, beep!

Mr. Pincus waved as he rolled by in his new EstateMaster golf cart, heading for the main office. Mom was in the passenger seat, with her easel and paints in the back. Mr. Pincus had hired her to do portraits of all the animals to sell on the new BushyTail website—and he was paying her a pretty penny!

I looked at my watch. I only had five minutes until I had to meet Mom in the parking lot. This was it. My summer job was over. It was time to say good-bye to Penelope. We didn't live in the same town, so I wasn't sure when the next time I'd see her would be.

Now, I realize that this is the point where stories can get really sappy. But I think you know by now that's not my style. So don't worry. You can put away your hankies.

But you have to admit that Penelope was pretty special, right? In just a few short months, she'd shown me how to soothe a flamingo, how to launch a raptor, how to capture a lemur, and how to rescue a lion. A pretty impressive list! In fact, considering that I thought the summer was going to be a total snoozefest, it turned out to be pretty wild!

"Say bye to your mom for me," I said.

"I w-will," said Penelope.

"And to Lila."

"D-Definitely! Her t-too!"

"See you next summer, maybe?" I said.

"M-Maybe," she said.

I turned around to walk down the path. I felt a little pang in my belly. And I felt like there was something in my eye. Darn it! I promised this wouldn't get mushy!

"Hey, R-Rafe," said Penelope, "I f-forgot. I h-have s-something f-for you."

Uh-oh. Now things were *really* going to get sloppy. Penelope had brought a good-bye present. Maybe a friendship ring. Or a flamingo feather. Or a lock of her hair.

I turned around.

"H-Hold out your hand," she said.

I did.

She gave me a dead cricket.

For most people, that might have seemed like a strange gift. But I knew exactly what it meant.

And I thought it was perfect.

ABOUT THE AUTHORS

For his prodigious imagination and championship of literacy in America, **JAMES PATTERSON** was awarded the 2019 National Humanities Medal, and he has also received the Literarian Award for Outstanding Service to the American Literary Community from the National Book Foundation. He holds the Guinness World Record for the most #1 *New York Times* bestsellers, including *Max Einstein*, *Middle School*, *I Funny*, and *Jacky Ha-Ha*, and his books have sold more than 400 million copies worldwide. A tireless champion of the power of books and reading, Patterson created a children's book imprint, JIMMY Patterson, whose mission is simple: "We want every kid who finishes a JIMMY Book to say, 'PLEASE GIVE ME ANOTHER BOOK.'" He has donated more than three million books to students and soldiers and funds over four hundred Teacher and Writer Education Scholarships at twenty-one colleges and universities. He also supports 40,000 school libraries and has donated millions of dollars to independent bookstores. Patterson invests proceeds from the sales of JIMMY Patterson Books in pro-reading initiatives.

BRIAN SITTS has collaborated with James Patterson on the *New York Times* bestseller *Two From the Heart* and *Kid Stew*, an award-winning TV series promoting creativity for kids. He lives in Peekskill, NY.

JOMIKE TEJIDO is an author-illustrator who has illustrated more than one hundred children's books. He is based in Manila and once got into trouble in school for passing around funny cartoons during class. He now does this for a living and shares his jokes with his daughters, Sophia and Fuji.